The House on Pope Lick Road

Laura returns home to settle the estate after her biological mother dies. Her journey uncovers how she survived and the protectors that made it possible.

The Road to the Pope Lick Trestle

Christine made a choice many years ago. Today, she is still living with the repercussions. She's left to ponder the randomness of the circumstances that took her down this path. Do you still call it fate when the outcome is tragic?

If not for him, she would have quit fighting a long time ago.

The Monster Under the Trestle

Evil surfaces in the woods surrounding the trestle. The final chapter in the series gives the protectors a final chance for redemption or condemnation.

The House on Pope Lick Road

Chapter 23: The Return to the Trestle

....A shudder came across me. The trestle shook a miniscule amount, but it felt like an earthquake to my body. The same vibration I had felt so many years ago. A train was coming. It was unmistakable. It would be here in a matter of minutes. We were close to the middle of the elevated span.

The vibration moved the tracks bringing Tommy out of his trance.

"Tommy!" I turned to him. "We must go back." I began to try and move away but he grabbed me with his right hand. He tossed the torch off the side of the trestle. It intensified my fear as the light seemed to fall forever. Tommy now had his left hand to gain an even better grip on me as I struggled to get away.

Our faces were close enough to feel one another's breath. Even in the darkness his eyes pierced mine with their cold stare. "We are finishing this. We are crossing this trestle." Both hands held firm on the front of my jacket as he began to take sideways steps in the direction of the train.

The tears flowed from eyes again as my feet were being dragged slowly in the direction of the oncoming train. I couldn't see the train yet, but I knew it was coming and coming fast. It was now or never. Tommy didn't come up here to cross the trestle. Tommy wants to die. Maybe even feels like he should have died twelve years ago instead of Luke. He was focused again on moving forward and dragging me with him.

I cleared my eyes with my left hand. I pressed the backs of the fingers on my right hand against the blade of the knife. I wanted to scream out from the pain. The blade extended in my pocket causing the handle and most of my hand to become exposed.

I slide my right hand down to firmly grasp the bloodied handle. I carefully withdrew the rest of my hand along with the knife out into the chilly night air. My right arm moved back even further to give me more opportunity to build momentum for my thrust at Tommy. Tommy's right side was exposed given his arms were raised as he continued to grasp my jacket at both shoulders. I quickly launched the knife with all my strength. It moved unencumbered until striking Tommy's side. It pierced his skin easily as it made its' way through his flesh. A loud cracking sound emanated from the strike as the knife penetrated through his rib cage. The knife came to a stop as the handle pressed against his side. All five inches of the metal blade were now inside Tommy.

Everything stopped for a moment. His eyes returned to mine. He seemed to be in shock as his head dropped to see my hand still pressed against him.

He started to fall but was able to keep his feet. Instead of continuing to drag me towards the train I felt a strong jolt as he pulled me towards the side of the trestle. He dragged me another few feet towards the metal rail of the train track. He shuffled his feet across the rail and was now just inches from the edge.

He looked back in my eyes. "I die, you die."

He was trying to pull me over the edge. I fell to give myself more leverage grasping onto the rail with my left hand. My right arm was still holding onto the knife I had jammed into the side of his body. Massive amounts of blood flowed out of Tommy's side. My entire arm was covered in it as he continued to try and pull me over the edge. Straddling the rail, I could feel the growing vibrations from the oncoming train.

I looked up at Tommy and screamed, "It was your fault!" I rotated my right hand twisting the knife in his side causing more blood to escape. He fell on top of me succumbing to the wounds inflicted by both Billy and me.

Tommy's head was resting on my shoulder. "Please, do not leave me out here alone to die." I gathered all my strength and pushed him off me.

"You chose this… I choose to fight." I turned and said to myself, RUN!

I looked over my shoulder to try and locate the train. The light from the engine was now visible. It would be on the trestle in a matter of seconds. I was at least three hundred feet from the clearing.

I ran like a child. I ran like I did running through the woods as a young girl. I didn't look back again for the train. Not even when a cacophony of noises rang out from the brakes being applied. I knew Tommy would soon be killed if he hadn't died already. My fear was replaced with a calming thought as I ran towards the clearing. With Tommy dead, Billy is safe. I did for Billy what I wished I had done for Luke. I did for Billy what he had provided for me all those years, protection. I had protected him.

The trestle was now shaking violently. I was still 150 feet from safety. The train whistle roared. I saw two orbs of light at the end of the trestle. Billy. They moved up and down once again as he readied himself to come out on the track to try and save me again. I screamed, "NO!" while sprinting towards him. I had to make sure he would remain safe. He heeded my request and knelt at the end of the trestle. I was now less than 100 feet from safety, but the train was closing in. The sheer power of the locomotive made my gait unstable. Billy lowered his head and began to pray. I was 75 feet from the end of the trestle. The light of the train was now illuminating everything in front of me. It wrapped around me showing the rest of the raised portion of the trestle. Billy was now clearly on display at the edge of the trestle. His lowered head made it easy to see blood on one of the two protrusions jetting out from his scalp. This must have been the residue of his attack on Tommy.

I could feel the heat coming from the train. I was less than 50 feet from Billy. I yelled out as loud as I could to overcome the noise behind me. "Billy, Thank You."

Billy's head raised, and his eyes widened. His expression confirmed my belief that the train was upon me.

I smiled at him as the train whistle blew one more time.

The Monster Under the Trestle

Chapter 1: The Protector
Chapter 2: Home
Chapter 3: Lance Corporal Jack Conway
Chapter 4: Searching
Chapter 5: Delilah
Chapter 6: A Day of Reckoning
Chapter 7: Hell on Earth
Chapter 8: The Aftermath
Chapter 9: Funeral Confession
Chapter 10: The Hunt Commences
Chapter 11: Peacekeeper
Chapter 12: The Sermon
Chapter 13: Notes
Chapter 14: Reunited
Chapter 15: Kindred Spirits
Chapter 16: Confession
Chapter 17: Collusion
Chapter 18: Last Rites
Chapter 19: My Story
Chapter 20: 10-64
Chapter 21: Condemnation and Salvation
Chapter 22: Emergence
Chapter 23: Words
Chapter 24: The Courier
Chapter 25: The Porch
Chapter 26: Huntington
Chapter 27: The Promise

Chapter 1: The Monster Under the Trestle

Three final words escaped my mouth as the unrelenting train was just inches from my back. "I love you." I wanted Billy to know he was loved. He is the sole reason I survived 12 years ago. He sacrificed everything for me.

Billy's expression changed over so slightly but fell short of a smile. The words could not replace the reality of what was about to happen.

Billy darted off to the side of the track despite my objections. Before I could scream no, I felt a blow to my back so forceful it took my breath away. It felt like I had fallen hundreds of feet and landed on my back. It was so violent my head snapped back until it slammed into the unforgiving iron frame.

The strength of the impact lifted my body and propelled it forward through the air. My arms swung frantically as they searched for something to hold on to in the darkness. In a moment, I would fall back to the track and be pulled under the wheels of the train. I closed my eyes and pictured my mom wrapping her arms around me.

Inches before landing, my forward motion changed suddenly to the left. Billy's outstretched arm was pulling me off the side of the trestle. The train continued barreling towards me. It contacted my legs which were now elevated behind me. It spun my body around forcing me off the side of the raised trestle. Billy had a tighter grip on my jacket than he did on the support beams. The two of us were now falling together off the side of the elevated train track.

My body was already limp from striking the train. Billy pulled me to him and wrapped his arms around me. Seconds before contacting the ground, Billy rotated our position placing me on top of him.

His back took the brunt of the impact from the 25-foot drop. I pressed into him as he absorbed my body weight. The pitch of the hillside, combined with the length of our fall, sent us both racing down the valley. Billy was once again protecting me from the jagged brush and rocky soil beneath him. The train above was still attempting to stop as we continued our decline.

Billy extended his right arm in search of anything to grab to stop our descent. The further we traveled the more damage was being inflicted on his body. Billy latched on to a small tree as we sped past it. The tree wasn't as tall as me but had enough of a root structure to counteract our inertia. Billy's strong grip made us swing around just below the tree before stopping our movement. The train above us did the same.

We stayed in that position for several minutes. I think we were both afraid to move. Afraid it would expose the seriousness of the wounds we had sustained. It was difficult to tell where all the blood was coming from. How much was from Tommy? How much came from either Billy or me? The moonlight was enough to see the dark patches on our clothing. The damage underneath remained hidden.

Various pain signals were reaching my brain. I moved my hand to explore the back of my head. My hair was matted together due to the blood escaping from the wound on my scalp. My back was experiencing the same amount of pain and yet I was grateful there were no sensations of additional blood flow. As worrisome as those injuries were, they paled in comparison to the growing concern for the lack of feeling I had in my legs.

My attention turned to Billy. He seemed disoriented. I moved my hand up to the side of his face. Fighting back tears, I tried to comfort him. "You did it again Billy. You saved me." I wasn't sure if we were ever going to make it out of the valley, but the truth is Billy gave me a chance. I stared into his eyes hoping he would respond. My mom flashed into my head again. I had stared into her eyes many times hoping for a reaction. I was beginning to feel lightheaded. My eyes closing and opening more rapidly with each second that passed. I felt myself drifting away.

"I save you." Billy uttered the words as he smiled at me. I smiled back and buried my face in his shirt. He gently rolled me off to the side of him. He sat up beside me as his fingers searched my body for the damage that had been inflicted. First, his fingers pressed against the back of my head. He removed them and brought them close to his eyes. He could see fresh blood was still emanating from the open wound. The only other blood he discovered was a laceration on my left leg near my hip. Whatever had torn it open had ripped my blue jeans with it. "We go, now. Not safe here." Billy was shaking his head as he spoke.

I looked up at Billy as I faded more from my normal consciousness. It was difficult for me to process anything that was happening.

"I take you home." Billy spoke again.

This brought my eyes back open again. "Home". I nodded. Home sounded perfect. Home is what I needed more than anything now. I needed to be held by my mom.

In one motion, Billy lifted me up off the ground. My head, arms and legs dangled below his grip. My eyes closed as my protector carried me away.

Chapter 2: Home

My eyes were pressed shut as I slowly fought to escape from a state of unconsciousness. Flashes of Tommy and the train rushed through my head. As much as I wanted to believe it was all a dream, the pain quickly reminded me of the trauma I had endured. My head felt like someone was standing on top of it. Like a vice tightening its hold with every turn. Tears formed in my eyes despite the fact they remained closed.

I was afraid to open them. Afraid to see the damage inflicted from both the train and the fall. Afraid to know where I was and how long I had been here. Wherever here is.

I noticed the sound of water dropping from a great height. It wasn't a waterfall just one drop at a time. It was extremely loud for such a delicate event. Every few seconds another droplet splashed down and replaced the silence with the robust sound. In a small way, it soothed me. It gave me something to focus on other than the pain.

It was then another sensation became discernable. My arms, face, back and chest were chilled by the cool temperature. There was a stillness in the air. No movement. Where was I? The thought didn't last long though, a new one hit me as hard as the train did on the trestle. My legs were not chilled like my upper body. In fact, I felt nothing from the waist down. More tears pressed against my eyelids.

One thing I could feel were the aches emanating from my back. My fingers explored the area around me. I felt a soft blanket underneath me. I extended my arms further from my side to allow my fingers a larger area to explore. They reached the end of the material and transitioned to a much different surface. It was hard and seemed to be covered in a thin residue of cold moisture. My fingers ran over the uneven ground investigating every detail. There was no grass, or dirt, for that matter. The cold and rocky substrate continued as far as I could reach. My heart rate started to elevate. A tear penetrated through my closed eyelids. It wandered down the side of my cheek leaving a trail quickly cooled by the surrounding air. It ran out of moisture before it reached the blanket beneath me. My mind was pulled back to my surroundings as another drop of water fell.

"Be strong Laura. Open your eyes." I whispered the words over and over until I had the strength and courage to move. As my eyes parted, only a small amount of light replaced the darkness. Everything looked blurry at first as if I were looking through a lens too strong for my eyes.

I pressed my fingers against my eyes to move the water and clear my vision. The view above me seemed to just fade into nothingness. It was difficult for me to know if this was a symptom of my compromised vision or the limited amount of light. No matter how hard I tried, I could not make out much directly overhead. I slid my arms back by my side to position my body for a better view of my surroundings. It took a great deal of effort to lift my shoulders a few inches off the ground. It also caused the pain to intensify in my lower back. My head tilted forward. I could now see the source of the light that illuminated the space. It was a candle just a few feet away. A little beyond the candle, a small creature crouched down at the edge of where the light extended. He was eating something and facing away from where I was positioned.

"Billy?" The name barely escaped my lips. The words prompted no reaction. He just continued to eat. "Billy." I said his name again this time with a little more strength.

He immediately turned still chewing his food. "You wake!" He scurried over to me dropping whatever was in his hands.

He could tell I was in even more pain trying to hold myself up. He placed his hand under the back of my neck. "West." His other hand moved just above my chest and applied a light amount of pressure. He wanted me to lie back. It didn't take much force to get me to succumb. He was now hunched over me with a smile on his face and tears forming in his eyes. "I save you! I knew you not leave me."

I didn't know how to react. I didn't even know where I was. "Billy, where am I?" I was terrified to hear his answer.

He smiled again before answering, "home." He must have known by the look on my face that I didn't recognize the space to be my home. "Bilwee's home. You safe, ba'low the bad men. Jus you and me. I dident need to get her. I do it all myself."

My head was spinning. "Get? Get who Billy? How long…" Billy softly covered my mouth with his hand.

"West." He started singing a nursery rhyme in his normal broken sentences. The drops of water splashing down between his words. The sound made me aware of my dry mouth and throat. My tongue felt like sandpaper against my lips. I reached my hand out to Billy and gently held his arm. "Water." I was only able to utter one word in my weakened state.

Billy smiled and seemed excited that he could do something for me. He quickly turned and moved across the room. A minute later he came scurrying back so rapidly he lost his balance and fell on my legs. The cup of water spilled just above my knees.

The whole incident happened so fast I instinctively arched up despite my condition. I could see the worried look on Billy's face. I saw the darkened area on my thigh where the water had soaked through my jeans. I began to smile.

Billy looked confused. "What Lawra?" He always had trouble saying my name correctly although his vocabulary and pronunciation had improved from when we were kids.

"I FEEL IT! I feel the coldness on my skin." Billy still looked confused. "I thought my legs were hurt really bad Billy, but now I can feel the water." I gritted my teeth and focused all my energy on bending my knee. It rose a couple of inches before falling back to the blanket along with my head.

"You did it! We play hidenseek." Billy jumped around knocking into me several times. I felt each blow. All the bumps confirmed I had full feeling in both legs.

I smiled seeing him so happy. It is how I remember him growing up. Before he learned his life was very different than every other child. Before he knew how much he had to be angry about. Before he knew how isolated he was in this world. I reached out again to get his attention. "Not yet Billy. I need more time."

Sad at first, a smile slowly returned to his face. He could see I was getting stronger. The expectation to be able to play his favorite game soon was enough to console him.

My body was failing me again. The effort of lifting my head and knee had drained all the energy from my muscles. My eyelids fluttered several times before closing. My mind reflected on the childhood game Billy and I would play in the woods. I exhaled one shallow breath as I drifted off to sleep.

"Billy!" I paused to allow the noise to disappear into the woods. "Billy!" I screamed out his name again as I hunted for him. "Where are you!" I hated playing this game with Billy. We played hidenseek almost every day since I met him a year ago. He couldn't even say the name of the game right. He ran it altogether like it was one word.

He hid himself so well it would take me forever to find him. He could be inches from me and still I could not see him in the brush. It became a boring and lonely game for me. I played it anyway because it made Billy feel good to be great at something.

It was Billy's birthday today. He was now six years old. The only gift he asked for was to play hidenseek. The simple request made it impossible for me to say no. I agreed to play several times today. After all, I have nothing else to give him for his birthday.

Billy could not run, or climb like me. His body was different. His hands and feet looked nothing like mine. It amazed me he moved as well as he did through the woods.

"Billy!" I shrugged my shoulders and fell to the ground among the branches and weeds. "I give up already!" My chin dropped to my chest.

I squeezed my doll between my arms. "Well Lucy, it's just me and you again until Billy comes out." I said it to taunt him. To get him to finish the game already. I knew he was close enough to hear me. He was always close. Anytime I stepped foot in the woods. Always within reach but hidden from view.

I closed my eyes.

The sounds from mother nature blended before fading away. I focused on the immediate area surrounding me. Silence. It was one of the things I liked most about the woods. Before I met Billy, I would go through this same routine. With my eyes closed, I could imagine almost anything. And almost everything I thought of was better than being at home.

Billy was going to pounce on me at any moment. I knew it was coming. It still took me by surprise when Billy sprung from the leaves. My heart jumped as his hands landed on my back. We rolled together several feet in a ball of arms and legs. Spread out side by side, our stomachs began hurting from all the laughter.

"Billy! You get me every time!" I sat up and playfully pushed him away.

He sat up and smiled back at me. "Agin, I hidenseek agin." He was now perched on his knees.

"Billy, I have to get home. Mommy will be mad if I am late." I hated saying goodbye to Billy. His smile always turned to a frown before I could finish saying it. Anytime I mentioned home he nearly cried. "Don't you need to go home?"

Billy shook his head side to side.

"Billy, where is your home?" Billy is my only friend. I get the feeling I am his only friend. It seems I may be the only person he sees most days.

A tear formed in his eye and slowly rolled down his cheek. "No howse."

His words made me sad. "Where did your mommy go?" I had met her once, a few days after I had met Billy, almost a year ago now.

Billy clearly wanted to talk about something else. His movements captured the nervousness building inside of him. His eyes darted away from mine as he looked around the woods.

I put my hand on his shoulder. The bones of his back were easy to feel given his wiry frame. I patted him softly to comfort him. "Don't worry Billy. I have a secret too. Maybe one day we can tell each other our secrets." I continued to rub his shoulder. He became very still as he leaned into my side.

I felt like Billy would stay in this position forever. He needed me even more than I needed him. As much as I wanted to be with him, I knew getting home late would upset mommy. I couldn't leave without giving Billy something to smile about.

"Home." My voice reflected the excitement I had for the idea growing inside of me. "Tomorrow we will start building you a home. I know the perfect place. A place in the woods no one ever goes. A place where I can always go to find you when I need you."

Before I finished speaking, Billy turned towards me and placed both of his hands on my shoulders. We moved together as our arms wrapped tightly around one another's back. I had hugged Lucy many times. This was different.

My eyes opened slowly as I awoke from the dream. It wasn't a dream. It was a memory. A childhood memory most kids think about all the time. I hadn't until now. The experience rekindled after seeing Billy again and hearing him talk about hidenseek. I had suppressed many memories from this time in my life, both good and bad.

I remember the house we built in the woods. We played in it almost every day. But the house we built was above ground, much easier for Billy to be spotted. Underground is how he managed to remain hidden all these years. This is the home his mother made for him to take refuge. It was a place he could be safe. It explains how he survived.

Billy was nestled in beside me. I had no idea if it was night or day. All I know is this was his real home. A home never discovered by anyone else. And for the first time in his life, Billy had someone to share it with.

Chapter 3: Lance Corporal Jack Conway

Date: October 10th, 1944

Dear Mom and Dad,

I trust both of you are doing well. Please do not worry about my well-being. We are making great strides under General MacArthur's leadership. I feel the tide is turning in our favor. I hope the recent events allow us to return home soon.

Our unit has just landed on the island of Peleliu. If we can take her, it will fortify our position and protect the Allied Forces from attack.

Dad, you would be very proud of me. They have increased my rank to Lance Corporal for my leadership and valor during my time overseas. To be honest, it is also the result of the many casualties we have endured. The enemy's bullets do not differentiate between the level of the service member they strike. We have lost many of our leaders, the majority of which I trained under and looked up to with the upmost respect. I will rely on my training and your influence as more men look to me for direction.

We have been assigned the critical orders to clear the underground bunkers in the area known as

Promontory. It seems recently the Japs have invoked a new tactic of battling from underground. If we are successful, we will destroy or render useless several Anti-tank guns that are taking quite a toll on our forces. It was an honor to have been selected but we all know the odds of successfully penetrating a significantly fortified stronghold. We are on their territory and they know it well.

Sir, I know you experienced many battles over the years while serving our country. I wish now that I had spent more time learning from your endeavors. I can only imagine how this may have helped me as we set off on the most challenging campaign we have been tasked to complete. I am confident in my training, but it is the leadership of the men where I feel I am a fraud. I hope my lack of experience does not undermine our mission.

Mom, my regret to you is that I did not write more since I have been away. Most of my unit writes letters daily to their loved ones. As you know, you have seldom received correspondence from your only son. I ask for you to forgive me for being deficient in this area. I must stay focused on the mission at hand. While some of my brothers write daily to their loved ones, it distracts me from what I must do and the clear head I must maintain. I hope you can understand my thinking on this issue.

It's time to get a few hours rest before we embark at 0600. Please keep my men in your thoughts.

Sincerely,

Lance Corporal Jack Conway

I folded the letter and placed it with hundreds of others in my bag. The truth is I have written many but only mailed a few. I knew the contents were too specific. They would never be cleared by the postmaster. Still, each one felt like a conversation with my dad. An experienced military veteran who understood a soldiers hopes and fears. Someone I could share with openly without creating angst amongst the men I lead. No one wants to hear a leader with uncertainty in his voice when the enemy is attacking. Writing it down allowed me to galvanize my resolve and lead my men effectively. I could explore the pros and cons of my orders guided by his voice inside of me. I hope one day to share them with my parents.

"Lance Corporal Conway, report to headquarters." I pulled the drawstring binding the top of the utility bag together. I tossed it on the other side of my cot. The men around me know what this meant. The mission was about to commence. All that was left was to review the objectives of the attack. My men readied themselves for battle.

"Yes, Sir!" I saluted the messenger and quickly passed by his side. I had awakened early and was already prepared for the day. I hastily made my way to the makeshift headquarters located on the beachfront we secured a couple of weeks ago.

"Sergeant Pike, I am reporting for duty." I saluted as I entered the room. Sergeant Pike was a strong leader of men. I had grown to like him even if I didn't agree with all his tactics. He was in his late fifties and had served for more than 30 years. He had a rebellious side. He would often challenge authority and even go rogue if he felt it was best for his men. I both admired and condemned him for this behavior. I struggled to know if it was a display of courage or blatant insubordination. I have learned, in a relatively short time, this is not as black and white as I would prefer.

Sergeant Pike reciprocated the salute as he looked up from the maps laid out in front of him. He traced his finger over the route we were to take to enter the man-made underground caverns. "Conway, once you get inside, we have only limited reconnaissance on the underground network. The bastards have carved out miles and miles of caverns. It's a maze of tunnels and fortifications. We do know the location of the submerged anti-tank guns. They have been firing regularly for weeks at our fleet. We believe we can access them through this tunnel. We have blasted it for days in preparation for the mission. Now is the time to commence with a ground forces and down those guns. Once inside you will have to keep the men on course. Chaos will no doubt envelope you and your men. You must push through. Our success relies on your success. Keep pushing until you have accomplished your mission or... Well Corporal, you know the drill. Keep your eyes and faculties about you, the Japs have traps hidden everywhere. Surprised they haven't killed all their own men with all the land mines they have placed in the tunnels." One thing I learned from Pike, and others like him, is to present the mission in a very matter of fact way. Do not get emotional and do not sugarcoat the reality of what is being asked. It would be a disservice to the men who are looking to you for leadership.

"Yes, Sir." I said it assertively to convey my conviction for what we were being asked to do.

"This is Lieutenant Steven Willis. He will be your commanding officer once you are out of reach of communications." I hadn't even noticed him standing off to the side of the large table. He stepped forward as I saluted him.

He spoke without looking at any of the maps or objectives listed on the documents. "We have three squads in our platoon. 36 total men. 12 Fire Teams like the one you command.

"Sir, why am I the only Corporal present for this debriefing? Where are the leaders of the other Fire Teams?" I seemed an inefficient method for conveying the mission objectives.

"Your Fire Team has the honors of leading the charge. Take your men into the cavern on the left. We will take the rest of the squad and flank your position to the right. If our intelligence is correct, we will rendezvous at 0700 about 1,500 feet inside the cave. From there, we know the anti-tank guns are approximately 1,000 feet to the south. The rest of the plan will have to be made on the ground once we see the terrain. This is not ideal, but we have no choice. We must stop those guns if we are to take the island and destroy the airfield. We have no idea how or if the caverns are connected. We don't even know how many divergent paths intersect the route. The anti-tank guns will be firing and that will be our guide." He stared directly in my eyes as he completed his overview.

My men were going in first. I was honored and terrified at the same time. Keep your wits about you I implored to myself. "Yes, Sir." My response was weaker this time despite my best efforts to conceal the concern growing inside me.

Sergeant Pike took back over the meeting. "The other Corporals have been informed. Return to your team and meet at the launch point at 0615." He saluted to let me know the meeting was over.

I returned the salute and did an about face to the opening of the tent. My first few steps were unbalanced until I steadied myself and grasped the importance of the mission. We must succeed. As I lifted the tent flap, I was greeted by a column of men on either side of me. 11 total. The 11 other Corporals that will take their three men teams into the caverns behind my unit. One by one, they saluted me as I passed their side. They had already been debriefed and came to show their appreciation. They knew my team faced an arduous journey through an unrelenting assault.

I walked past them with a sense of purpose and a pace to match the intensity of the situation. The only good news in the whole affair is the little time we had to mull over the orders. I now had to return to my Fire Team and convey the mission to my men.

I entered the tent that housed the four of us. My men were already prepped and standing at attention. They were a reliable and trustworthy group of men. All three just 18 years old. They looked up to me, even though I was just a year their senior. Yet their age did not show in their actions. They battled valiantly in previous confrontations and their reputation reflected their success. I hoped in some way my leadership contributed to the results we had collectively achieved. And now, I must look them in the eye and instill confidence in the mission knowing we were about to die. I knew the odds and I knew what we were being asked to do. We were chosen because of our grit. We would not turn back no matter how much our enemy threw at us.

"Private Sanders, Carter, Epps." Already at perfect attention, hearing their names lifted their bodies even more. "Our mission is simple men. Enter the cavern first and clear the way so others can destroy the anti-tank guns." I paused to see if there were any signs indicating the scope of the mission was more than they could handle. None of them flinched. "Very well. We leave in ten minutes. Fall out!"

The men went about their business of preparing for the attack. I reviewed the initial assault route through the cave where at least some intel existed. I had already committed the route to memory, and I knew the men had been over their equipment multiple times. The activity and routines kept our minds from wandering. I peered up at the men to check on their demeanor. Private Carter had ceased his equipment check. He had retrieved his stationary and writing utensil. I made my way over to his bunk. His pen had yet to touch the blank piece of paper.

I placed my hand on top of his, "Now's not the time Private." He looked up at me standing over his left shoulder. My men need to be focused on the mission at hand. This distraction so close to the attack could only hinder our resolve. "Write when we get back."

"Yes sir." He complied, immediately returning the personal items to their appropriate place.

The mission was at-hand. I gave the command to fall in.

We marched with our usual precision to the rallying point. Lieutenant Willis saluted our Fire Team as we approached. The allied forces were already launching a massive attack to draw attention away from our mission. The sound of mortar shells exploding were something you grew use to over here. Silence is now what I feared hearing the most.

I took my men to the fringe of the cavern and the newly discovered access point. Private Epps began to retrieve his military issued flashlight. "Private Epps, replace your flashlight."

"But sir, how will we see once inside the cave?" He had a confused look on his face.

I looked at each of my men as I responded to his reasonable question. "The light will draw fire to our exact location. We will be sitting ducks in there. Remember this is their land. They know every inch of it. They will have sentries posted despite the cover fire from the other allied forces. Our only advantage is to stay hidden as long as possible."

Epps has always respected leadership and I knew his concern was directly related to the magnitude of the mission we had been assigned. Still, I could see my answer did not completely relieve his concerns. "Epps?"

He looked down before responding, "how will we know where we are going?"

Another fair question. "I have the route memorized. Each of us needs to stay in physical contact with one another. We will scoot and shoot if needed. I will keep us on track with occasional calibration checks. I will use my zippo lighter under cover at various checkpoints to confirm our path."

Epps expression changed to one of determination. "Yes, sir." He knew I was prepared. He knew I had considered every scenario before we even stepped foot in the cave. The exchange renewed his confidence in the mission.

Crouched behind a small ridge the opening was just a few feet away. If the enemy was positioned inside the cave, we would be picked off before we even knew what hit us. Our advantage is the cover of dark. To this end, I gave the following order to my men without explaining the reason. "I am going in first. Wait here for five minutes." I looked at each of them for a response.

With a little reluctance they each responded, "five minutes."

"Good. If all is quiet, enter the cave in five minutes." I nodded again at each one of them to confirm the order.

I started to move out from behind the ridge when I felt my pack being pulled from behind. I turned to see Private Carter's hand grasping the material. Before I could protest his actions, he simply said, "Good luck Jack."

It wasn't appropriate to call an officer by his first name, let alone put your hands on him. Nonetheless, I appreciated the overture. "Thank you, Adam." My men rarely saw me break protocol and the exchange seemed to ground each of us.

Private Carter released his grip as I moved over the ridge. I was completely exposed in enemy territory. I stayed close to the ground as I crawled into the opening of the cave. The morning sunlight faded from view as I slithered into the darkness. The temperature dropped suddenly just a few feet into the cavern. I moved slowly over the uneven surface to reduce the risk of making a commotion. Each reach of my hand could be my last should I trigger a hidden mine to explode. I made my way far enough inside the cave to give all three men room for cover.

I waited. Listening. Silence. There were either no Japs positioned in the area or our intel was correct, and any resistance would be encountered further inside.

My men did well. Not only did they wait the exact amount of time, but I did not hear any of them as they crawled to my location. The opening was not visible from our location as the cavern had a pretty extreme bend to the right. This was probably man made to keep the fortress better protected from artillery. The result was the complete absence of light. It was so dark, Private Sanders crawled into me before coming to a stop. As instructed, Epps and Carter were right behind and maintained contact. From this point forward, all four of us would move as one.

We continued our descent into the underground cave. We moved at a snail's pace to avoid taking a wrong turn, or worse, accidently tripping a land mine.

We heard the other Fire Teams enter the cave. They were not as cautious as my team. They could be heard from 50 feet away. Their path was soon to diverge from ours. I felt better about my team going alone given the commotion in which they entered.

The cave returned to its serene state once the members of the other 11 teams had veered off to our right. It was now that I could begin to hear the muffled explosions from above our position. Like thunder off in the distance, the rumbling was distinctive yet carried with it a new fear. Could the cave system collapse under the intense bombing of the Allied Forces? It was a thought best kept at bay as we continued further into the cavern. The bombing provided additional cover for our movements.

I huddled under my drop cloth every five minutes to check our position. The material hid almost all the light coming from the flame. I estimated we had moved about 1,000 feet in the past 25 minutes. We still had another 500 feet to go to rendezvous with the other units.

I turned to my Fire Team, "Men, we are nearly to the rendezvous point, but we must increase our pace. We cannot have them reach the location first. We cannot have them take the first attack or we risk failing our mission." I couldn't make out their faces. I couldn't read their expressions. They knew we were a decoy. Sent to draw fire so our reinforcements could determine the exact location of the enemy. And yet, they followed me dutifully as directed.

I quickened the pace considerably with my men closely behind. The aggressive movements inflicted more pain from the sharp rock edges we scrambled across. What once sounded like thunder off in the distance was now much louder as the bombing was almost directly overhead. We were getting close.

A different sound whizzed past our position. It was the unmistakable sound of a bullet flying past our heads. I never even heard the gun fire. Just the bullet flying by and crashing into the rock wall behind us. We froze in our tracks. Was it just a random scare tactic or had our whereabouts been noticed by the enemy? A minute passed with no additional shots fired. We had no choice. We had to move on despite the potential danger lurking ahead.

"Bang, Bang, Bang…" a rapid fire of bullets sprayed the area around us. I kept my head up long enough to determine the location of the gun fire. The flashes from the last couple of rounds gave the enemies position away. The bullets were not close to hitting us. It was clear he could not make out our movements. "Bang, bang, bang…" Another round fired in our direction. The flashes all came from the same place. It was most likely a single soldier tasked with making first contact with intruders. Undoubtedly, his job included relaying an attack to reinforcements further inside the cave. We must take him out before he had a chance to signal for help.

I turned to the men and quietly said, "charge." I sprung up fast almost pulling Private Sanders off the ground with me. We began a steady jog as we widened our line. We stumbled across the uneven surface moving forward side by side. "Fire!" We unloaded our weapons lighting up the dark cave.

Return fire raced past us much closer than before. There was no hiding now. Each of my men saw the target and continued the assault.

I issued a cease fire order confident our attack had killed the enemy. I pulled Sanders down to the ground. He grabbed Epps on his way bringing all three of us crashing to the surface.

We had lost contact with Carter. No gun fire returned from the original location. I whispered loudly, "Carter." No response.

As I readied myself to get up to search for our fourth team member, fire erupted from the other side of the cave opposite of where we had fired before. There was either a second shooter or the first gunman had survived and moved locations. The bursts of gun powder lit up the cave and gave away Carter's position. He was now ten feet in front of us and still standing. He returned fire until he screamed out. He was hit. In between the flashes, we saw him fall to the ground. All three of us stood up in unison and launched a massive counterattack.

"Cease fire." I commanded loudly to halt the onslaught.

The cave became silent. The rumblings from overhead began to build again muffling all other sounds. I knew they hadn't stopped, our ears just needed to adjust to the closeness of the recent rifle fire. I instructed the men to stay in their position before crawling forward to check on Carter. His moans were growing louder as I approached his side. I flipped my lighter on to determine the extent of his injuries. As I brought the lighter close to his side, more shots rang out in our direction. This time the jap was charging in our direction.

Epps and Sanders returned fire given I was in a compromised position. The enemy was an easy target as if he intended to be shot making a valiant, albeit futile charge.

He dropped to the ground just a few feet from where Carter was lying on the ground. I resumed the medical assessment of his wounds. I started at his head as the lighter flickered side to side. The flame bounced around as my hand shook nervously. There were no signs of injuries to his head as he turned to look at me.

"Lance Corpor…" I brought my finger up to my mouth to silence him. It was bad enough the lighter was acting like a beacon for gun fire. Our two faces were just inches apart. I could feel the heat of the flame from the lighter on my face.

I quietly responded, "I'm here." I moved the lighter down to his chest and noticed the first wound. A bullet had pierced his chest as evidenced by a tear in his uniform shirt and the darkened stain of blood around the entry point. It was above his heart but difficult to tell the extent of the damage.

Before I could continue, Sanders and Epps crawled up to my position. I didn't have time to address them. I also knew my words would be wasted given they just saw their unit member fall. My hand moved further down to Private Carter's stomach. Three more wounds came into view. I ended my examination. There was no reason to continue. The bullets had ripped through enough of his body tissue that he would bleed out in a matter of seconds. Sanders and Epps dropped their faces into the ground upon seeing the condition of their friend. I took the light back up to the Private Carter's face.

I was conflicted. We needed to move to give the mission any chance of success. We were also sitting ducks if our movements were relayed to others in the Jap army. Reluctantly I implored the men, "We need to move."

Their heads rose in unison and the flickering light exposed the look of disbelief on their faces. Sanders broke the silence, "we stay with Carter."

I fought the urge to pull rank with my Fire Team members. Sanders voiced exactly what I was feeling inside. And yet, it is easier for Sanders to take this position. He does not carry the responsibility of the other men when he makes his decision. The three of us stared at one another with no words being exchanged. It was clear they were not leaving Carter in this condition.

Our attention returned to our fallen soldier. He was struggling to breathe, gasping as if someone was covering his mouth with a towel. I knew he didn't have long. "Adam, what did you want to write in your letter?"

Tears were now running down his face as he continued his curt and violent gasps. I wasn't sure he was going to have time to respond. "My little brother..." he gasped again almost choking on the fluids that were building in his lung.

Sanders started softly saying the Lord's prayer. He could sense he was fading.

Sanders continued praying as I re-engaged Carter. "What do you want me to tell your little brother?" I fought back my own tears not wanting that to be his last memory. I nodded at him to encourage his response and feigned a smile.

His lips pressed together as he swallowed deeply. "Tell him… Tell him – I'm sorry." He struggled to get the words out.

Epps and Sanders were now watching as their friend was nearing the end.

I did my best to fill in the gaps and give him some peaceful resolution. "What are you sorry for Adam?"

More tears streamed down Private Carter's face. A few escaped my eyes as well despite my best efforts to withhold them. "I am not going," he gasped before continuing, "to see him again." He turned away from me before barely getting out a few additional words. "I promised him."

Epps and Sanders shuffled to the other side of their fallen team member. I could feel his grip weakening.

Epps put his arm around his head and pulled him to his chest. He whispered in his ear, "You will see him again." Epps was crying as he tightly embraced Private Carter.

A minute went by before I placed my hand on Private Epps shoulder. "He's gone." We had all seen this often but rarely was it this close and never someone we knew as well as Carter.

Private Epps released his colleague acknowledging Carter had died. Carter's head fell back to the cave floor as Epps buried his face into the chest of his fallen unit member.

I placed my hand on his shoulder and had to do the most difficult task a leader will ever face. I had to convince the remaining two members of my team to complete the mission. "We have two choices." I paused still trying to put the words together. I struggled with the right course of action and even more so how to articulate it given the circumstances. They were looking to me though and I owed it to them to lead us out of this hell. "We can stay here with Turner and live knowing his final act will be part of a failed mission." I moved my lighter closer to both men's faces to look into their eyes. "Or, we fulfill our mission, help protect the other men in our platoon." I paused again before finishing, "and, be able to tell Carter's little brother he died on the mission that wiped out anti-tank guns. He died part of the unit that changed the course of the entire war. That is the message I want to deliver when we land state-side."

Epps wiped his face clear of the tears and nodded affirmatively. They were friends but they were also soldiers.

The decision was made for us as another round of bullets flew past our bodies. Sanders had just finished praying when the popping sound filled the

cavern. He stood up and yelled out, "Die you Jap…"
His words were cut short as bullets riddled his body.
We returned fire snuffing out the shooter.

We quickly turned to Sanders. Unlike Turner, he was
already gone. The only consolation is he suffered far
less than his team member. I looked at Epps and
restated the need to move, "Go!"

We passed four fallen Japanese soldiers. The result
of the intense gun fire we had exchanged. It gave us
no comfort.   If all we do is kill four Japs our mission
will be a monumental failure. Our end goal is to save
thousands of lives.

It appeared the enemy troops failed to get a message
to reinforcements. We would have encountered many
more troops if our attack was communicated up the
chain. The noises heard in the cave were now
coming from underground. The proximity of the anti-
tank guns drowned out the explosions overhead. We
were getting close to our objective.

We made it to the rallying point before the other Fire
Teams. Despite the unexpected delays, we had to
wait for the rest of the Platoon to arrive. No words
were exchanged as we remained hunkered down
behind a rock wall. I am sure Epps was reflecting on
the life and death of Private Carter and Private
Sanders. Each of us dealt with the past 15 minutes in
our own way. The military family is an amazing thing.

We only knew them for about 9 months. Still, we were as close to them as anyone in this world. Their deaths were a reminder of how fragile life is in war. At any moment, we could join Carter and Sanders and never take another breath.

It was once again easy to hear the rest of the Platoon as they closed in on our location. Lieutenant Willis approached first. He crawled up to our position. "Report."

"We met some resistance. Killed four enemy soldiers. We do not believe they relayed our attack. We need to re-stock on ammo. And, we lost Private Carter and Private Sanders." Saying it out loud made it seem real. It also made me question my leadership. As if I were admitting mistakes to my commanding officer. I felt particularly responsible for Sanders death. Had I maintained our readiness; Sanders would still be with us. I lost two men when I could have had the blood of only one soldier on my hands.

The news took Lieutenant Willis off guard. He looked at the two of us. "We knew this mission was going to be difficult. Let's finish it so we can return to base."

We reloaded our weapons and restocked our ammo. We now had the rest of our Platoon at our back. We met little resistance as we moved towards the anti-tank guns. We may just complete our mission after all.

The next few minutes were a blur of forward movements mixed with a barrage of gun fire. One Fire Team was completely annihilated thanks to a Japanese booby trap. The explosion blew several other Platoon members off their feet. It was challenging to keep track of one another given the elements. We just kept pressing forward.

As we closed in on the Anti-tank guns it was heavily fortified as anticipated. Each remaining service man in the Platoon retrieved a grenade as instructed by Lieutenant Willis. A coordinated launch of twenty-six grenades were sent into the large underground room that held the guns. We covered our ears and crouched behind a ledge to take cover. It was the loudest explosion that I had heard in all my time serving in the war. The force blew past us illuminating every inch of the underground network of tunnels and caverns. Fire continued to burn on everything except the rocky surface of the cave. A few survivors ran past us in the cave searching for anything to douse the flames. They quickly fell to the ground overcome by the injuries they sustained.

What looked to be a daunting task had ended with much less resistance than we anticipated. We fortified our position and ensured the Anti-tank guns would never fire on Allied Forces again.

We would spend only one more night on the island of Peleliu. There were just the two of us left in the tent.

We didn't sleep and for most of the night we remained in our bunks in complete silence. The anti-tank guns were not firing and conversely, we were not firing on them. It was almost serene tonight on the beach front. A small reprieve from this godforsaken war.

Private Epps broke the silence softly saying out loud, "Why did Carter make that promise to his little brother?" There were no tears or sounds of distress detectable in his words. I believe both of us had nothing left inside of us after the past six hours.

"Carter was a sheep more so than a lion. He should have never been on the island of Peleliu. None of us should have been here for that matter. I don't mean to impugn him. Not at all. It's just, he was the most genuine individual and caring soldier I met in this outfit. He couldn't have known what it was really like when we stepped foot on those transports over a year ago. We heard the stories, but you don't believe it until you're here. And then it's too late. He became the best soldier he could be for someone with such a kind heart." I stopped to see if Epps would respond. "Get some sleep Epps, tomorrow we have to be lions again."

Epps turned on his side and maneuvered his blanket up close to his shoulders. As dutifully as always, he respectfully heeded his superior officers request.

I on the other hand pulled stationary out to draft a letter. It was less than 24 hours since the last one. This was atypical for me. I wasn't writing to my parents though. Instead, I addressed the letter to the home of Private Carter. The letter recapped the entire mission. Private Carter died a hero. The second letter I scribed was to the home of Private Sanders. It contained the same mission detail and heroism of the letter to the Carter family. It also included an apology. An apology from a young Lance Corporal that reacted poorly in the heat of battle. I went against my training and it cost us a good soldier. I wanted his parents to know. I finished the letter and closed my eyes. I whispered my commitment, "never again." Never again, would I let emotions distract me from the mission and the men. Never again would I allow another soldier to be in harm's way because of my inaction. I said it out loud one more time, "never again."

Chapter 4: Searching

"Christine." Margaret shook my arm to get me moving. It was Sunday morning and the chores needed to be completed before church service. Fortunately, Simon excused my attendance at Sunday mass some years ago. I think he knew the risk outweighed his desire to see me conform. It didn't stop Margaret from asking. "Do you want to attend church with me?"

I am not sure why she continued to ask. My spirit had been broken a long time ago. For a while I tried to separate the words from the messenger. The scriptures helped the first few years. The longer I stayed in the Divine Commune, the more difficult it became to reconcile the two. The evil actions of Simon and his two brothers were too much for me to resolve. I had spent twenty years in this world, and it had beaten me down. I always justified my inaction because of Billy. It is a miracle he was born and even more miraculous he somehow survived to become an adult, at least chronologically. I could have abandoned him years ago. Either ran away or taken my own life. There were times when I nearly ended it. Ended the pain from the physical and mental abuse I had endured since I got into Jeremiah's truck so many years ago. Every time the same thought entered my mind. I pictured Billy. A boy so disfigured many would not even glance his way. If they did engage him, they would persecute him for something completely out of his control. But he was my son, and I loved him. I always will. I sacrificed everything to give him a chance to live. This is the only thought that gives me comfort. I shook my head side to side to confirm what Margaret had to have already known. I was not stepping back in that church ever again.

The last few years have been extremely difficult. I seldom see Billy. The few times I have seen him he seemed different. Nervous. Anxious. It only heightened my concern for his well-being. He is the reason I am still here. It saddens me to not see him as often as I did when he was younger. I lethargically make my way through each day awaiting my next chance to see him. Months and months have passed with no contact. I tell myself he is grown now, and it is normal for him to be on his own. But nothing has been normal about our situation. We only had each other for most of our lives. He had his friend Laura when he was a child, but the last 15 years I have been his only companionship.

Not attending church gave me a larger window of time to visit Billy. I would go each Sunday morning hoping he would be waiting for me. Hoping to have an entire hour to spend with my son. Most Sundays, I just sit in the underground sanctuary all alone. I take one small candle with me each time. Each minute in the cave would pass excruciatingly slow. As the light faded, I knew it was time to return or risk being discovered.

I watched through the window as Margaret and Jeremiah left for church. The next ten minutes were the happiest moments of the entire week. It was the time it took me to make my way to the well. The hidden entrance to the cave just a few feet further. Each step I took was a little faster than the last. I was almost sprinting by the time I reached my destination. I prayed I would see my son today.

I went through all the precautionary steps to enter the cave. I could do each of them with my eyes closed after so many years. It is a small miracle my activities went undetected right under the watchful eyes of Simon and his two brothers. It was a testament to the attention to detail I undertook with each visit. My motivation was always the same. If they discover the entrance, they discover Billy. If they discover Billy, all is lost. I removed the brush from above the entrance to the cave and retrieved the wooden box that was just underneath. The wooden box contained extra candles and matches, an overcoat and strips of material that could be used for a torch should the need arise to go deeper into the caverns. I placed the large overcoat over my clothes to protect them from the elements. The coat was quite worn but still did its job. Part of the illusion was to be able to return home with my clothes in similar condition as when I left. As I moved just inside the entrance, I placed the brush across the top hiding my whereabouts. I descended into the dark canal. The reward at the bottom was a breathtaking Sanctuary hidden under the earth.

Sanctuary, the name I had given it not only because of its beauty, but also because it was a place where my thoughts were mine. Simon couldn't control me in the Sanctuary, and no one ever put a hand on me down here. To enter the Sanctuary, you had to navigate the four foot drop out of the cavern. It was now a routine maneuver given all my practice. Once my feet were on the ground, I held my breath as I lit the candle. Light began to penetrate through the cold air across the vast openness of the chamber. I stepped forward so the light could touch the farthest reaches of the space. Nothing. Billy was nowhere to be seen.

I took my usual place on top of a folded over blanket in the middle of the underground room. I leaned back against the natural rock formation that extended toward the ceiling. My eyes closed and my thoughts centered on Billy. This was the longest length of time I had ever gone without seeing him. As much as it scared me, I may have to search the caverns and beyond the wall of the Commune to reach him. I was much younger when I last attempted to reach the woods. I drifted off to sleep, overwhelmed by the physical endurance such an endeavor would take on my body.

My eyes opened as wide as they could go. My body began to shake. I had forgotten to replace the wooden box under the brush. It was exposed to anyone that came near the area. Perched on the hillside like a beacon flashing to attract attention. The consequences of my error so significant it awoke me from my nap. How and why this thought entered my subconscious is beyond me. I slowly turned to see the amount of wax feeding the flame of the candle. There was so little wax left the light flickered furiously. It could extinguish itself at any moment. I had never forgotten to hide the box in all these years. I hurried to climb to the opening and fix my mistake before it was detected. The overcoat was only half on my shoulders when I lifted myself up into the shaft. My heart pounding as I scratched and clawed my way up the ascent. I came to a sudden stop. I heard the unmistakable sound of footsteps redistributing leaves just a few feet above my position. I retracted to remain hidden completely in the shadows. I waited. Praying the brush covering the opening would not be discovered.

The footsteps moved even closer before stopping. I heard the latch being rescinded on the wooden box. The sound of the top landed with a thud against the crunchy leaves that covered the earth. The items were being shuffled around creating more noise. That's when I heard Margaret's voice call out. "Jeremiah, what are you doing down there."

Her scream had to be an attempt to warn me. It was louder than the distance required for Jeremiah to hear. The name reverberated through my head rendering me paralyzed.

"Someone been up to something." Jeremiah always spoke in truncated sentences.

Margaret did something she's been doing for years. Protecting me at her own peril. "I left it there yesterday. I thought I heard something in the woods and completely forgot about when I returned to the well. I am so absent minded." She expressed the last few words with a sound of exasperation as if to dismiss it as no big deal.

Jeremiah's feet shuffled as if he turned in the same place. I assumed he was now facing Margaret. I crawled forward to see if I could make anything out through the branches and leaves that hid my location. It was difficult but it appeared he was standing a few feet to the left of the opening facing back towards the well.

He responded to Margaret, "and what need would you have of candles and matches in the woods?"

Margaret did not miss a beat. She answered almost as soon as Jeremiah finished talking. "I had just made some new candles for the cabin. I was letting them dry in the clearing so we could use them at night. I wondered where I had left those."

I waited to see if Jeremiah believed her cover story. "And this old pocket watch? What need could you possibly have for that?"

The pocket-watch! My hand went to the pocket of the overcoat. It was empty. The pocket watch came in handy to time our excursions. Time. Time was always the greatest concern when we visited the caves. Underground time always seemed to pass faster than the agonizingly long seconds that ticked off above ground while in the Commune. The pocket watch saved me on hundreds of occasions. Simon and Jeremiah loved their routines. Any deviation would draw attention and that was never a good thing. The watch must have fallen out into the chest when I put it on earlier. How was Margaret going to explain the purpose of the watch?

"That's mine. Brought it to make sure I was back in time to start dinner." Margaret was good. Her voiced never wavered. She had me believing her story and I knew it was not the truth.

Nothing happened for a minute. I heard leaves shuffling again. A few small leaves and sticks penetrated the brush covering and fell around me. My hand went over my mouth. I shuffled a few feet further down the cavern. It sounded like Jeremiah was still inspecting the area for additional clues. He didn't seem to trust Margaret. Never really has since I've been here. God knows I've seen her take so much abuse over the years over his skepticism. Even when she tells the truth, she faces his wrath.

"CRACK!" A large branch snapped. It felt like the whole cave was collapsing. All the brush pushed into the opening filling it from side to side. Jeremiah clumsily landed on his back as the back of his head struck the hard rock surface. I feverishly began moving the brush and uncovered a boot. It was Jeremiah's left leg. I heard more leaves rustling around as Margaret approached.

I was just starting to emerge from the large amount of debris when she spoke. "O God, is he dead?" She stood above me motionless.

I stared up at her. "I don't know!"

Margaret did not budge. Her body immobilized at the site of Jeremiah wedged into the opening of the cave. She remained perfectly still, despite my pleas for her to check on her husband.

My only option was to do something that was so revolting it almost made me physically sick. I had to crawl over top of him to check on his injury. Each movement across his body made me cringe with resentment. I hoped he was dead. He deserved to die years ago. His body did not react to any of my movements even with all my weight pushing down on him. I forced my back against the rocky surface behind me to minimize the physical contact. The passage narrowed causing my face to drag across the front of his flannel shirt as I moved upward. I stretched my arm forward and pressed my fingers against his neck. I had to push through the thick facial hair that extended far down under his shirt collar. My chin pressed into his chest as I watched for any sign of movement.

I noticed a subtle rise and fall. It lifted and fell ever so slightly. At the same time, I felt the unmistakable movement of blood moving through his artery. It was weak but it was there. It was horrific. Here I am positioned across his large, slovenly body and he could awaken at any moment. I could now see a small stream of blood flowing from the back of his head. Landing on the rock must have gashed him pretty good. Still, I worried that any movement might bring him out of his unconscious state. He could crush me with just one of his hands given his size and my frail body. I looked up towards Margaret. I said nothing but my expression conveyed my helplessness.

She moved her head side to side as if she had no answer.

My shoulders slumped. The fear in my body overtook any hope I had in getting out of this alive. I may have just given up the one thing that has kept me going all these years. Hiding the path to Billy. Jeremiah and his brothers would search every inch of the underground caverns. They would eventually find the room he grew up in. See all his makeshift toys and drawings. The discovery would push them to the other entrance. An entrance deep in the woods where Billy's above ground home is located. They wouldn't stop until both of us were dead.

Tears started rolling down my eyes. I stared up at Margaret. "Please Margaret. I need you right now."

My plea worked. Or at least it got her moving. She made her way to the opening and crouched down. She was now just inches from Jeremiah and not much further from me. "Slide back down Christine. Pull his legs down the descent. I'll push from up here. We need to get him to the Sanctuary. We can figure it out from there."

I allowed myself a small amount of relief. Margaret continued to be in my corner. Even with her husband severely injured in the fall. The relief was short lived as I had to slither back down across his body to reposition myself beneath him. I nearly threw up as my face brushed against his body. My neck straining to hold my head sideways away from his clothing. I was full of contempt once again.

I made it beneath him and began to pull with as much strength as I could muster. I could barely see Margaret over Jeremiah's protruding stomach. There were only a few inches of separation from the top of his body to the top of the cavern. Margaret had made her way just inside the opening and was pushing on both of his shoulders with her feet.

His body moved inches at a time with each exertion. We found a rhythm to our movements expediting our descent. Thankfully gravity was on our side. Without the downward angle of the entry canal, we would never have been able to move him.

My feet dangled over the opening into the sanctuary as I continued to tug on his leather boots. I placed my feet flat against the wall just below the opening. I pushed off as I pulled violently on his legs. I fell backwards as my hands lost their grip on his feet. The aggressive movement caused me to land with a thud on my back. The candle continued its fight and was somehow still providing light. Half his body was now visible in the sanctuary. I made my way back up to his legs that were left hanging down from the opening. I took each boot under each armpit and closed tightly. I called out to Margaret, "when I count to three push with everything in you! One, two, three…"

We timed the movement perfectly. For as much as he weighed, he moved swiftly out of the shaft. His head took another blow as it fell to the rocky surface. I was thrown back on my bottom with his boots still tucked under my arms.

Margaret poked her head out from the opening. She reached out with both arms down the wall. She obviously did not want to waste time climbing back out to come in feet first. Jeremiah was positioned beneath the opening cutting the usual four-foot drop in half. Her hands made it to his chest to allow her to continue safely moving into the sanctuary. Her hands walking down the front of his body as her feet were still above her. Her face conveyed the same disdain at having to touch him. Even though they were married all these years, the abuse had taken its toll. Her legs stretched as far as they could before falling out causing her to roll off the side his body.

We both sat up amazed we had moved him down the passageway.

"C'mon. Margaret implored me to get moving." She was becoming much more assertive in responding to the situation.

I moved to the other side of the Sanctuary to retrieve a rope to secure him. I made my way over and came to a stop. The rope was still tied to the makeshift crib that used to contain Billy when he was just a baby.

"C'mon already." Margaret was getting impatient and rightfully so. Jeremiah would very well kill both of us if he awoke.

I hurriedly untied the knots while thinking of my precious son. I hadn't seen him in so long and thinking back to when he was an infant brought tears to my eyes. I missed him so much. I needed his strength now. His survival instincts.

One more knot to go. My fingers started to fail me as I heard the groan from across the room. I turned to see Margaret had begun to move slowly away from where Jeremiah was lying. My hands trembled making the untying of knot even more challenging. Another moan. Please, please, give me this one thing. Give me this one thing for all that I have endured. Tears were now streaming down my face. I used my shoulders to wipe my eyes every few seconds to clear my vision. Another moan came from across the room. I turned again to see if there was any movement. Margaret crouched down against the wall of the cave with her head between her knees. I returned to the knot. My fingers slowed their movements, the knot began to release its hold. The rope whipped from around Billy's crib as I turned to move back to Jeremiah.

I hollered to Margaret. "Help me!"

Her head sprung up to see I had freed the rope. She shuffled towards Jeremiah. We both reached him at the same time. His eyes still closed but he was beginning to make small movements with his legs and arms. He started moaning again, this time continuously.

"Behind him." I motioned to Margaret to move to behind his head. We both squatted down. "Push him up." All four of our hands wedged under his shoulders as we strained to raise his upper body off the ground. Once high enough, I slid my knee under to prop him up. His head dropped forward helping our cause. The entire back of his neck was covered in blood that had streamed down from his wound.

Margaret brought his hands behind him overlapping his wrists. His latest moan sounded like he was trying to talk. Like he had marbles in his mouth. We were running out of time.

I quickly began weaving the rope around his wrists and lower arms. I overly tightened the knots not caring if I was inflicting any pain. His grunts and groans were growing louder and more forceful. "His legs." I moved my head towards his feet. Margaret just looked at me. I screamed at her, "tie his legs with the other end of the rope."

I finished securing his arms as Margaret moved down his side pulling the rope with her. She frenetically began wrapping it around his right ankle. I continued pushing my knee in his back, holding his arms behind him.

Jeremiah started convulsing his body. He was becoming more aware of what was going on around him. He yelled out, "you are just like Delilah. Betraying me!" He was staring at Margaret as he said it. Veins in his head could be seen given how much he was straining to get a hold of her.

I tried my best to restrain him. I placed my arm around his neck and pressed the inside of my elbow against his flesh. I placed my other hand on my forearm and tightened my hold even more.

He struggled and shifted side to side moving me with him. Margaret tried to secure the rope around his left ankle to bring his legs together.

Jeremiah lifted his left knee bringing it towards his chest. I held on trying to secure him. It all seemed to move in slow motion. Margaret lunged forward to grab his leg in another attempt to restrain him. As she moved forward, he extended his leg violently. His boot landed in the middle of Margaret's chest with such force she went sprawling across the Sanctuary. She landed awkwardly several feet away before coming to a stop.

I held on for dear life not wanting Jeremiah to make it to his feet. If he made it to his feet, he could kill Margaret with one kick.

Jeremiah continued kicking both legs out in front of

him. I pressed my body against his arms that were now pinned to his back. He grunted out in pain as spit and saliva ran out of his mouth and down my forearm. His hands were able to reach my thighs given I had raised up to exert more force. He dug his fingers into the muscle. They pressed against the bone as I yelled out in pain.

I couldn't take it anymore. I lunged forward crumpling him in half. He kicked more slowly as the extra pressure on his neck forced him to succumb. Even after he stopped moving, I held on to ensure he was out. I kept my arm around his neck as I placed his shoulders back on the ground. No movement. I released my grip. Blood now covered the overcoat and parts of the white dress I had on underneath. I quickly made my way to his feet finishing what Margaret had fought valiantly to do just moments earlier. The rope grinded together as I pulled it tightly. His two legs now braced together as one.

I crawled towards Margaret not knowing what to expect.

Chapter 5: Delilah

"Margaret!" I gently shook her shoulder hoping she would respond. I leaned over her and put my cheek near her mouth. I would give anything to feel air moving against my skin. I wrapped my arms around her and pulled Margaret to me. This woman had made sacrifices for me since I arrived at this evil place. Margaret also knew my story. My whole story. She knew about my dad and how much he loved me. She knew about Johnny. She knew Johnny was the closest thing to a fairy tale moment in my life. She knew about Billy and all the efforts we both made to keep him safe from the Commune. She was the only one who knew me. If she didn't make it, it would make me that much closer to having never existed.

I cried into her shoulder and held her close. "I have not always kept the faith like I know I should. I know you may have been testing me and I failed you. Margaret has always believed. She continued to look to you even in the darkest of times. Please do not take her this way."

"I'm here teeny." She whispered into my ear the nickname my dad had given me so many years ago. I hadn't been called that in a long time.

I slowly pulled away so I could see her face. I looked into her eyes and nodded. "We did it. We fought off Jeremiah and saved our lives." Her expression changed suddenly as she looked across the room at Jeremiah. I knew what she was thinking. Now what? "I don't know." It was an honest answer. She needs to be the one who decides. It is, after all, her husband and the father of her children.

Margaret began to sit up but hesitated as the pain in her ribs overwhelmed her. "Help me." She reached her hand out in my direction.

I clasped my hand around her wrist and gave her the extra support she needed. We both were now sitting next to each other looking over at our captive.

Margaret broke the silence. "I need time to think." It was easy to tell she was thinking through multiple scenarios in her mind. "I need to get back. I need to check on Thomas."

Thomas was her youngest child. He was a teenager now. Her oldest, Ezekiel, had grown into a young man. He was just a little older than my Billy. Ezekiel always looked out for me just like Margaret. It's hard to imagine he came from Jeremiah. It was a good thing he took after his mom. "You're right. We need to make sure they do not connect you with Jeremiah missing. "I have a change a clothes I kept down here for emergencies." I looked directly in her eyes. "Are you strong enough pull this off? You know Simon will interrogate you. He will become enraged when he learns his brother is missing."

Margaret nodded. "I've had years of practice masking my feelings."

The words reinforced the pain and suffering this woman has endured for so many years. I wish I could have done more to shield her from all of this. "Why did he call you Delilah?"

Margaret gave a half smile and responded. "This is why you should go to church with me." She let out a nervous laugh but stopped herself as it increased the pain in her chest. "Delilah betrayed Samson. Had his hair cut while he slept. His hair is where his strength came from."

The stories from the bible always confused me. I could never determine the intended message. Simon had contorted the stories for years to fit his narrative and support his actions. "What happened to her."

Margaret raised her eyebrows with an expression of bewilderment. "No one knows for sure. She is never mentioned again in the bible. Some believe she was killed when Samson got his revenge."

Still confused about what to take away from the story, I returned my focus to the matter at hand. "Margaret, I don't know how this is going to end." I had to see if Margaret had considered the only viable option in my opinion. "I do know we can never let Jeremiah leave this cave. If it comes to it, I will do what is necessary to protect all of us." I waited unsure of how she would react.

She nodded just once. I closed my eyes knowing the gravity of the statement I had just made. Margaret turned away, "I need to go."

I retrieved the clean clothes and gave her the overcoat to protect them on the climb as she exited the cave.

Before she started her ascent, Margaret turned back to me. "You know what this means. You can never come back to the Commune." It was hard for her to get the words out of her mouth. Even though we had both suffered while living in the Commune, we persevered because we had each other.

I swallowed and answered, "I know." I didn't want to acknowledge the reality of the situation. My choices were to live in the caves or attempt once again to escape through the woods. Billy spent his entire life in the woods. I am not even sure he would go with me now. Even if he did, would he be accepted outside the only world he has known. How could he possibly fit in? How could I after all these years?

The immediate concern was dealing with the next few hours. "Go, before they notice you being gone. Act like you know nothing about Jeremiah. Or me for that matter. We went missing. Return when you can and only if it is safe to do so. I will be fine." I gave her the most confident and reassuring look that I could muster. The last thing I wanted her to worry about was me. She would need all her focus to convince Simon she had nothing to do with Jeremiah's disappearance.

We hugged one another again as Margaret scurried up the passageway. I could hear her repositioning the brush to cover the entrance. She spent extra time doing so given the pending intensity of the coming search efforts. Simon will search every inch of the Commune. He won't stop there. He will exhaust every resource at his disposal. His man hunt will extend to the woods that surround his property. He will leave no stone unturned. He had proven his conviction many times before.

Chapter 6: A Day of Reckoning

Margaret left leaving me alone in the Sanctuary with Jeremiah. Normally it would be terrifying to be alone with this man. It seemed different now. I had all the power. The ropes were secured. I even took one additional measure by tethering him to a rock formation. Even if he somehow made it to his feet, he wouldn't be able to go far.

There I sat across the room contemplating my options. What I really wanted to do was make him pay. Pay for putting me in that vehicle so many years ago. Pay for drugging me and transferring his evil acts to Billy while he was still in my womb. And pay for the years of abuse he had inflicted on Margaret. A smile spread across my face. He thinks of himself as Samson.

I went into the caverns to Billy's old home. He hadn't returned to the room in years. I believe he preferred living above ground so long as it was safe. Over the years, I had stocked his space with almost everything he could need and that would go unnoticed by those in the Commune. I remembered I had given him a pair of shears. They will work perfectly to shave the bastards head.

I made it to his room by virtue of a makeshift torch. Before I stepped inside, I looked further down the cavern. Down there was the way out. A path I had tried many times. I dropped my head knowing another attempt would be coming. It was a sobering thought. I had broken bones, cuts, bruises and many scars from all the failed attempts. I also had my darkest day in the underground passage. The day I had lost hope and considered ending my life. Billy kept me going even when my will had been broken.

I stepped into his childhood home. Even though I didn't go there often, it brought back good memories from my past visits. All the stories and songs we sang together raced through my mind. You would have never known we were in a cold, dark cave. It was the warmest place I knew as an adult. It's where I was a mom to my son. It was my home. It was more of home than the cabin I shared with Jeremiah and Margaret.

I immediately noticed something very different as the light illuminated the room. Someone had been here. Someone had been here recently. Many of the items were gone. Picked over as if it had been looted. There really wasn't anything of great value other than the sentimental connection I had with each item. I fell to my knees both saddened the items were gone and wondering who had taken them. Did someone find Billy? Is that why I haven't seen him? As a mother, the worst thoughts flooded my mind. I searched around frantically for any indication of what may have happened to Billy.

I came across a few of the pictures we had drawn together and some of Billy's old clothes. The small size brought back memories of when he was a young boy exploring the cave with me. I closed my eyes hoping and wishing he was okay.

I searched some more and found the shears. It reminded me of why I came here in the first place. I collected a few things and made my way back to the Sanctuary. Once I dealt with Jeremiah, I would do whatever it takes to find Billy.

Jeremiah was still out of it as I entered the Sanctuary. I must admit, I felt quite devious. I strolled over to him and positioned myself beside him. I grabbed a handful of his matted hair and lifted his head off the rocky surface a couple of inches. No response. I began to shear away most of the hair on his head and beard. It was very patchy as I haphazardly made my cuts. I then opened the shears and used the inside of the blade as a razor to shave off the remaining hair. The edge of the blade was notched with many nicks from all the years of use. It left numerous small cuts across Jeremiah's head, face and neck. I didn't slow down my movements even while shaving around the now congealed wound on the back of his head. As I was finishing, he started to moan like he had before.

I scuffled back even though I knew he could not hurt me. I waited for him to awaken. Chunks of his hair were strewn about him as he began to turn his head and move his body.

"Margaret!" He screamed out before opening his eyes. He seemed discombobulated. Tears started falling as he began to blink. "Margaret!" The second time was just as loud. It was a good thing sound did not escape the depths of the Sanctuary.

He moved side to side awkwardly given his hands were secured behind him. Jeremiah continued to cry and shake as he became more conscious. He finally lifted his head to see me smiling at him. He looked around the cave. His expression let me know he now remembered how he got in this position. The shoe was finally on the other foot and he knew it.

I decided to have some fun at his expense. I needed to pass the time anyway. "So, you fancy yourself to be the big strong Samson. Huh?" His head dropped back against the rock. I was shocked to see him continue to cry. He knew it was me. The same person he viewed as being weak and inferior until now. And yet, he cried in front of me. Cried like a baby. "Maybe you are Samson. Seems cutting your hair has made you an even weaker man." I raised up on my feet and made my way over to him. I leaned over and swept up a large handful of his trimmed hair in my hands. I positioned myself above his head and slowly let strands of hair fall over him. The last few follicles floated down as I swiped my hands back and forth together. I began walking in circles around him smiling at his fall from power.

My taunts were getting to him. He started to wrestle more as he tried to move freely. He was inflicting more pain on himself with each thrust. It didn't take long for him to realize his attempts were futile.

He glanced over and noticed the rock formation where his rope was fastened. He contorted his body to inch over to the structure. It was very entertaining. I laughed out loud watching him struggle. The laughter echoed through the caves making it sound like an entire crowd was heckling him.

He somehow managed to shimmy his way up the formation into a seated position. All the effort took a toll on his energy. His chin dropped to his chest from a lack of strength.

Tears continued to flow down his nicked-up face. The salt in the liquid made him winch each time it penetrated the hundreds of tiny cuts. The fluids combined and spread across his face making him look like a deranged clown.

I stood over him to demonstrate my knew found power. I also wanted him to strain his neck to see me. He lifted his head high as he could to see my smiling face looking down on him.

He finally spoke between sniveling outbursts, "Samson's…" He stopped and started his sentences multiple times before finishing each thought. "Samson's hair grew again." He smiled through the tears and whimpering. "Sampson regained his strength." His pupils were now in the very back of his eye socket as he stared up at me. It exposed an unnatural amount of the white of his eyes. "Did you know that? Did you know he returned and killed everyone in Ashdod for their sinful ways?" A wicked smile stretched across his blood-soaked face.

I laughed again to mock him as I held the shears into the air, "well, I guess we can't allow your hair to grow back." I opened and shut them several times releasing the sound of the metal blades gliding across one another. "You forget I attended the same church you did for years. I was listening. Never spoke, but I was listening."

Groggily, he stuttered through a response. "Ah woman, what the hell are you talking about."

I opened the shears as wide as they would extend. Dropping to my knees, I moved closer to him. I placed the blades on both sides of his neck. His breathing labored causing his skin to move up and down against the sharp edges. He knew any movement would likely create a mortal wound. I stared into his soulless eyes and calmly restated a bible passage Simon shared years ago. "Ezekiel

34:16, I will seek that which was lost, and bring again that which was driven away, and will bind up that which was broken, and will strengthen that which was sick: but I will destroy the fat and the strong; I will feed them with judgment." I emphasized the last two sentences as my voice reflected the turning of the tables. "You see Jeremiah, we can all use his words to justify our actions. Not yours or the perverted interpretation your evil brother spouts from the alter each week. It will be up to him to decide our judgment. And he will have to decide how to reconcile my actions after I kill you." I pulled the shears back leaving two new wounds stretching across his neck

His head dropped and his moans increased. I felt no remorse for this man. I know we are supposed to forgive people when they sin. But it is not in me to do so. There is nothing inside of me now to guide my actions. The emptiness hardened my resolve and made my decision an easy one. I will kill this man for all that he has done. If this condemns me to hell, then so be it. I had plenty of experience with pain and suffering in this world. Could Hell be all that much different?

My heart jumped when something touched my shoulder. I quickly darted a couple of feet to the left. The shears fell from my hands clanging against the hard surface. I knew Jeremiah was secured across the room but still my heart was racing. I slowly looked up to see what caused the disturbance.

There stood Billy.

My hand covered my mouth as I moved to embrace him. I wrapped my arms around him and squeezed him tight. "Billy, I thought I may never see you again." I held him close and refused to let go.

"Mawmee. It okay." Billy tried as usual to comfort me.

Reluctantly, I separated from the embrace. He was just a few inches from my face. I could tell something was different about Billy. Even after having not seen him in a couple of years, I could tell. He seemed happy. He seemed content. I stared at him wanting this rare moment to last forever.

It didn't. The moment was severed by piercing laughter from Jeremiah. It was obnoxiously loud and annoying. My attention on Billy had caused me to completely forget he sat just a few feet away.

Billy and I were both now looking over our shoulder at the monstrous sized man tied up across the room. Billy pointed in his direction, "Bad man. I hear him yewl at you."

Jeremiah continued laughing increasing the amount of blood emanating from cuts on his face. "Your son.

That thing came out of you. You had that bastard…"
He stopped short of finishing the sentence while
pondering the word that would inflict the most pain.
"Animal!" His laughter followed immediately after the
last syllable left his mouth.

I turned to Billy. It was always my greatest fear.
Having my son accosted by others that would not
accept him based on how he looks. It's why I kept
him in the woods.

The expression on Billy's face was changing. His lip
quivered ever so slightly. Rage was building inside
him. Billy had come to protect me. And now that he
saw the slovenly man taunting me, he wanted even
more to avenge me.

Billy began to move towards Jeremiah. I reached out
and grabbed his shoulders. "No, son." I couldn't let
him get involved. This was my day of reckoning, not
his.

Billy continued staring at Jeremiah as I pleaded with
him to go. "I will come for you. I will find you. Give
me one day to deal with this and I will come for you."
Billy slowly turned back to me as I finished reassuring
him.

Jeremiah's laughter was roaring in the background,
but it faded away as I looked into my son's eyes one
more time. "I will come for you. I have so much to

make up to you. I love you son. I have always loved you."

A tear dropped from Billy's eye, "I know mawmee." Billy glanced back at Jeremiah before giving me another hug. He unwittingly made his way to the tunnel and stopped. He lifted his hand and waved once in my direction before leaving.

I watched him disappear just as quietly as when he entered the room and touched my shoulder. I placed my hand on the same spot where he had touched me. I wanted to remember the contact I had with my son.

The loudness of the laughter never subsided. I was growing more aware of it as Billy faded from my thoughts. How dare this man mock my son after all that he has done. I picked up the shears and clasped the closed blades between both of my hands. The metal point extended 5 inches beyond the end of my fingers. I held the shears up to my face so Jeremiah could see them.

His laughter was now intermittent. Fear began to refrain his audacious behavior. He began to shake his head side to side as he yelled out. "Psalms 37:8, cease from anger and forsake wrath, it is not wise to do evil. Cease from anger and forsake wrath. Cease from anger and forsake wrath." He continued repeating the broken message from the bible passage.

I took no heed of his words or actions. I began to charge at him. I would thrust the cold blade into his chest with all my force. I lunged at him and extend both arms as the blade moved to within inches of his chest. He closed his eyes and tilted his head back as if to look to the sky for someone to intervene. The tip of the blade contacted his chest. My hands slid forward down the shaft of the blade to the very end of the point. My hands were now pressed against his chest still holding the shears. Only the very tip had penetrated his skin.

I couldn't do it. As much as I hated this man, I could not bring myself to kill him. My head dropped beside the shears as I began to cry. Why didn't I have the strength to finish him. I knew I let my son down and my lack of action could put him in harm's way.

I lifted my head to see Jeremiah had opened his eyes. Six inches separated our faces. I looked into his eyes. It was almost like I saw through them. I knew he was a soulless man who hid behind the true tenets of the bible and its teachings. His eyes conveyed the evil within him.

Something came over me. I lifted the shears back to my chest. I worked my fingers back up the blade to expose the metal point again to Jeremiah. I prepared to thrust them deep into his chest. As I moved forward, he countered by launching his forehead directly at mine. The shears were just inches from piercing his chest when his large forehand smacked into my skull. It immediately paralyzed me. The shears dropped between us as I went limp and fell to the side. My head felt like it had split in two. I laid on my side as I looked up at Jeremiah.

He began to laugh again. "You, you weak, woman." I couldn't move. I saw him shuffle around trying to secure the shears with his hands tied. He moved up and down violently causing my body to rise and fall as I remained stretched across his legs. I closed my eyes hoping it would all be over soon.

Chapter 7: Hell on Earth

I felt like I was floating. Swaying side to side in the air. My head was throbbing. My shoulders felt like they were being pulled out of my arm sockets. I opened my eyes to see I was dangling several feet off the ground. My arms were behind me and fastened to my ankles. It was an unorthodox position causing pain throughout my body. I arched my neck to get a better view. It caused me to swing at a greater rate through the air.

Jeremiah was no longer tied to the rock formation. He must have worked himself free with the shears. Not only had I not killed him, I had given him the tool to escape.

The sound of footsteps could be heard circling around me. As much as I tried, I could not see him. My movements caused me to swing even more ratcheting up the pain as the rope pulled on my wrists and ankles. He was teasing me.

"Good. I wanted you to be awake for this." Jeremiah leaned close to my ear as he uttered the words. I felt the heat from the torch he was holding. He moved it under me placing it on the ground of the cave. The flames reached towards me within inches of my neck and chest. I could feel the heat blistering my skin.

Jeremiah extended another unlit torch into the flames beneath me. As the material caught fire, the flames moved closer to my skin. I screamed out in pain.

"Good. Scream as loud as you can. Call that bastard son of yours back to the cave." I want you to see his demise before you pay for your sins.

Billy. My son. I must protect him no matter what happens to me. I will not give Jeremiah the satisfaction of a response to anymore of his torturous actions. I clenched my teeth together.

Jeremiah removed the second torch and walked beside me. He kept the flames inches from my body as he left my line of sight. The heat moved down my body before stopping at my knees. His sinister voice filled the Sanctuary. "Psalms 55:15 – Let death seize upon them, and let them go down quick into hell; for wickedness is in their dwellings, and among them." He said it slowly and loudly as if he was preaching to a congregation.

He moved the flame up to my exposed feet. I felt like my skin was melting. I wanted to scream out again but knew Billy would answer my call if he heard me. I closed my eyes and did my best to ignore the excruciating pain.

"Her feet go down to death; her steps take hold on hell." Jeremiah continued his biblical taunts. As if his actions were justified by words he did not fully comprehend. He removed the flames from my feet. The burning sensation continued for several seconds. The burnt flesh odor filled the room.

The pain was causing me to lose focus. I could feel how close I was to passing out again. Maybe it would be for the best. Die as peacefully as possible in the Sanctuary. The room that had given me shelter, safety and the little hope I held onto all these years.

Jeremiah's footsteps were moving from where I was held. I heard the pale I kept for water scrape across the ground before being picked up. Jeremiah returned and removed the flame from under my chin. It was a brief respite from the heat. He placed both torches out in front of me a good number of feet before moving back by my side. My body almost went into shock as he emptied the cold cave water across my back. The contrast from the heat to the cold was extreme. It took my breath away. I gasped audibly as I struggled to resume a normal breathing pattern. It sent me rocking back and forth through the air searching for oxygen to fill my lungs.

It was clear he was moving back across the Sanctuary to refill the pale with more cave water. I began to convulse from the chilly cave air. My clothing kept the weight of the frigid water pressed against my skin. I remained quiet though. Still driven to protect my son.

Jeremiah returned with the bucket in hand. "You will be in hell soon for all your sins. This is just a taste of what is to come." He retrieved one torch with his free hand. He brought it close to my face. I turned as much as I could to shield my skin from the flames. "You thought it was amusing when you cut my hair." He stopped intentionally to allow the unknown to increase my anxiety. "I am not good at cutting hair. I don't have the patience for that." He cruelly paused again. "I will just burn it off you." He brought the flames within a few inches from the side of my head.

Quietly I pleaded with him, "please, please stop." I looked up at him hoping he would show me mercy. There was no sign in his expression that he would cease until I had no life left in me. He knows about Billy. The secret I have kept hidden for all these years. He will hunt him down and kill him. I have let every loved one I know down. My father, then Johnny, and now my most precious reason for living, my son.

Jeremiah moved the torch even closer. It was impossible for me to tell now if my skin was on fire or if it was just the residual heat coming from the flame.

"Stop!" A familiar voice called out from across the room. We both turned to see Margaret had entered the Sanctuary undetected. She was holding Jeremiah's shotgun and pointing it at his chest.

Jeremiah was frozen in his place just a few feet from me. He broke the silence with his usual abusive tone. "Really, and what do you think you are going to do with that woman. You need to go. This is no place for you to be. GO!" He screamed the last word.

Margaret took a step forward to demonstrate her resolve. She calmly responded, "actually, this is our place. You are the one that doesn't belong here."

It was apparent that Margaret was not fooling around. Jeremiah fell to his knees and just as quickly as before began to grovel and cry for mercy. He really was a weak man hidden in the body of a much larger person.

Margaret took aim. I hoped she had the strength to pull the trigger. The strength I lacked moments ago. I stared at her from my tortured perch in anticipation. She could save my Billy. Save him for good from this man's reach.

Jeremiah between tears made a desperate plea. "The boys. Think about our children."

Margaret pressed her finger against the trigger and responded. You could see the whites of her knuckles as she gripped the gun tightly in her fingers. "I am."

She pulled the trigger and the Sanctuary lit up like a carnival ride. The bullet moved swiftly through Jeremiah's body before his mind knew what happened. The blood splattered all over me as I had no time to look away. Jeremiah remained kneeling as the blood poured from the exit wound on his back.

He finally succumbed to the injury and fell back over his feet. He stared up at me as the last breath left his mouth. The expression in his eyes remained unchanged. They were as empty as they were when he was alive.

Chapter 8: The Aftermath

Margaret held the gun longer than was necessary. She kept it pointing at Jeremiah's crumpled up body as if she expected him to rise from the dead. I gently swayed above him. I closed my eyes to avoid staring into his lifeless expression.

I heard a loud noise from where Margaret was standing. I turned and opened my eyes to see she had discarded the gun. It had landed several feet away from her like she had thrown it through the air. Both her hands moved to cover her face. I had no idea of how to respond to what just happened. I felt ashamed that she had to do what I failed to do. A wife and mother had to take her husband's life. The father of her children. Even if he was an evil man, I believe the reality of the situation was setting in. She had taken another person's life.

I lowered my head as the strain added to the pain I was feeling throughout my body. Margaret must have noticed my movements.

I heard her footsteps approaching. She took a roundabout path to avoid getting too close to Jeremiah's body. She retrieved the shears and made it by my side. I felt her hand lightly move across the skin of my exposed feet. The same burnt flesh from just minutes earlier. The movement caused me to jerk forward even though it was a gentle touch. I was shifting forward and backward again at an accelerated pace. I felt Margaret's arm reach around me as she stopped my movement. She positioned her knee under my chest for more support. I heard the shears open.

Soon, I would be free of the rope that restrained my entire body.

I felt a kick in my ribs as I began to sway even more frantically than before. Margaret screamed out. I tried looking over both shoulders, but the swift movements made it impossible to see what was happening.

I could hear Margaret moaning loudly. All other noise in the sanctuary had subsided. I lowered my chin to my chest hoping to see more from a different angle. I was in shock at what came into view.

Billy was perched atop Margaret. The bloody shears were in his hands.

"Billy." I called to him. He turned to me with a boyish look on his face like he had done something wrong. "Cut me down, now!" My strong words made him move. As he lifted off from Margaret's body, she moaned even louder.
Billy slowly made his way over to me and began using the shears to free my arms and legs. The movement of the blade across the rope made me swing even

more. I was feeling nauseous. What did Billy do? It all happened so fast. I never even heard him enter the room.

My legs fell first to the ground of the cave. Billy had not thought to brace me as Margaret had with her knee. My feet hit the cold rock sending radiating pain through my legs. I dangled by my wrist now twisting in the air with my knees, shins and feet dragging across the bumpy surface of the cave.

Billy continued to work on the final rope restraint. Margaret's moans were getting softer. The sound was replaced with Billy crying. It made his movements choppy which in turn made it take longer for him to free me.

"I sauwwy mawmee." His cries continued. "I thought she hurt you." With the last word my hands fell from the rope bindings.

I placed my hand on his cheek before hurrying over to Margaret's side. The front of her dress was soaking up the blood from the wound. The blood stain was growing. It looked like a dry sponge changing color as it pulled the fluid from beneath it.

I turned to see the frightened look on Billy's face. I was still in shock that he returned to the Sanctuary. "Billy, why, why did you come back? I told you to go."

His head dropped to his chin. "I sauwwy. I huwd the gun. I hate guns." He gritted his teeth as he said it.

He came back for me. He saw Margaret standing over me. I was bound like an animal. He was only trying to protect me.

"Son, go, I will come for you." I tried my best to reassure him. He did not need to see this. I know he is not prepared to deal with such things. His mind is much simpler. There is right and wrong. And he thought Margaret was doing something wrong. "I know you were only trying to protect me. Go. I will find you soon."

His tears slowed as my words sank in. His shoulders lowered, knowing on some level, his quick action was not warranted. He awkwardly made his way to the tunnel before disappearing into the darkness once again. Billy was so familiar with the caves he did not need a torch to navigate them.

I returned my attention to Margaret. I pressed some cloth against the wound on her chest. The pressure caused her to grimace. She doesn't have much time. The shears penetrated her small frame to a significant depth. "I'm so sorry Margaret."

Margaret's hands made their way on top of mine. She used what strength she had left to grasp them firmly. "I got to see Ezekiel and Thomas grow up. I saw them become young men." She paused between each word as less and less blood carried oxygen to her vital organs. "I know they can now be free of the evil presence of Jeremiah." I thought it might be the last words she ever spoke. I lowered my head just beside hers until our cheeks were touching one another.

This woman had cared for me while I was in the Commune at her own peril. She sacrificed so much for me over the past twenty years. Her last action saved me and my son. I had no words to convey the love I felt for her. I squeezed her hands in mine and told her simply, "I love you."

A few seconds went by as I held the embrace. Margaret's fingers were no longer gripping my hands. If I let them go, I feared they would fall by her side. I held on.

Much more softly than before, Margaret uttered a few final words. "Be with your son. Go to him. He needs you more than ever." The emotions overwhelmed me. Tears began to roll down from my eyes and move from my skin to Margaret's cheek. I shook as I held her. Our cheeks sliding across each other's, lubricated by the fluid from my eyes. After several minutes, I gently kissed her on her cheek. I lifted my head and looked into her eyes. They conveyed the warmth and caring nature of her soul even though she had passed.

It took me several minutes to find the strength to let go of her. Her last words were the same as so many other times over the years. Selfless and inspiring. She didn't blame Billy, even though he had caused the wound that took her life.

Standing in the Sanctuary, I was reminded of all that had taken place. The ropes still swinging from side to side, Jeremiah's body crumpled over in its place, and Margaret lying not too far away.

I needed to get to work. There was much to be done to hide the evidence. There will be a search. Three people have gone missing. If it were just Margaret and me, Simon would probably search us out with his own posse. Jeremiah's disappearance is a whole other thing. Simon will use whatever resources at his disposal including the police. He will exhaust every inch of the area. I need to get rid of anything that might encourage them to track Billy. If they find the Sanctuary, it needs to be a dead end.

The task would not be an easy one. First, I need to dispose of Jeremiah. I knew the perfect place. One of the tunnels off from the Sanctuary led nowhere. Except at the end was a large crevice with a significant drop. The water had carved out the rock over centuries of time. At one time, I thought this might have been my path to escape. The steep decline and endless drop made it impossible to traverse. Given the depth below the surface, it was doubtful that it led anywhere anyway. It was about forty yards from the sanctuary. This would typically only take me seconds to traverse but now I would be dragging a huge man behind me.

I faced away from his body and picked up a leg in each arm. I had no desire to look at him ever again. I snuggly held each boot up to my shoulders as my arms wrapped around them. His ankles pressed into my arm pits on each side. I stepped forward as his body moved a couple of inches. I lowered my stance to get more leverage. This was going to take some time and much of what little energy I had left. The sooner I clear the scene, the quicker I can seek out and reconnect with Billy. This motivated me to push through the pain and get moving.

I alternated tossing the torch further down the tunnel and picking up his legs to resume my movements. I know he is dead, but still it repulsed me to touch him. I took some satisfaction in knowing his head continued to bounce over each hard rock protrusion as we moved.

It was an arduous journey that gave me time to clear my head. I was becoming more confident about what I had to do. This wasn't the case for most of my life. I was being controlled for so long, the feeling of being in control felt good. I reached the precipice of the crevice and fell to the ground. As difficult as it was to drag his body, it may be more taxing to push him into the hole. I avoided looking at him as I made my way behind him. I closed my eyes and placed my fingers under his shoulders. In one motion, I lifted his head and shoulders off the ground while sliding my knee underneath him. He was propped up in front of me. I leaned into him some more causing his upper half to fold over towards his knees. The only thing that kept him from folding in half was his large stomach. I pushed again as I grunted out loud. His body rolled onto its side with his head inching towards the opening. I continued to push off with my legs as I slammed my shoulders into his side and back. His head was now disappearing into the expanse. I pushed again and he slid into the crevice up to his stomach. His robust waist blocked his passage. His legs were still resting outside of the opening.

I couldn't help but start to laugh. It wasn't right. You are supposed to have a certain amount of respect for the dead. I covered my mouth like I did when I was a child in school after being told to be quiet. The more I tried to squelch the laughter, the louder it got.

I stared at the half-exposed body not sure what to do.

I began to kick at his back side causing him to inch forward. My laughter continued as it became a game. I would stomp on him wondering which impact would send him cascading down. "One, Two, Three!!!" I chanted with each kick. "Go where you deserve to be!" And then it happened. His overly large stomach passed through the opening and the rest of his body quickly followed behind. I heard several impact sounds as bones cracked and crunched on his way down. I put both hands over my mouth to smother the laughter. I did it. I may not have pulled the trigger, but I had a great deal of satisfaction knowing he would never be found. He would never have the hypocrisy of a funeral service. And his sinister brother, would go on the rest of his life not knowing what happened to him.

As much fun as I was having, I had one more task that would be much more solemn. I had to do something with Margaret. She doesn't deserve the same fate as Jeremiah. She deserved better.

.

Chapter 9: The Burial

The torch lit up the room as I entered the Sanctuary. I sat it on the ground and crouched down into a ball just a few feet from Margaret. The emotions of the past few hours overwhelmed me. I dropped my head to my knees as my arms wrapped around my shins. The tears continued to flow from my eyes. How many tears can one-person cry? The only way I could stop them was to focus on Billy. Where did he go and how was he doing? He killed a person. Something I couldn't bring myself to do just hours before. I knew he needed his mother. I could already sense the guilt within him. My immediate reaction in the moment after he attacked Margaret probably added to his confusion. As chivalrous as his intentions were, he had killed a sweet and innocent person. A person that had experience just as much abuse as Billy, or me, for that matter.

I lifted my head and looked at Margaret. She didn't deserve to be drug across the cold, rock surface and dumped down a hole. And yet, I lacked the strength or tools to move her in a more respectful way.

I leaned over Margaret and wrapped my arms around her. "I am sorry for what I have to do."

Her final words inspired to me to move. She pleaded for me to go to my son before she died. She knew he needed me now more than ever. Margaret knew her fate and knew how it was going to end for her. This gave me a small amount of justification for taking actions that I would never do under any other circumstance. It isn't close to what she deserves but it was the best that I could do.

I worked my fingers around her back until I connected each hand together. I pulled up but my strength failed me. I was growing weaker from all the energy I had exerted dealing with Jeremiah. I could only lift her a few inches before returning her to the ground. I dropped my head to her chest and felt defeated.

I felt a tapping on my shoulder. This time I wasn't startled. I knew the touch was that of my son. I looked up slowly over my shoulder. "Billy."

"Mawmee. I help." His expression conveyed a more mature person than I had ever remembered seeing. He knew he did wrong and he knew he should help make amends. He even took charge of the situation and motioned for me to step aside.

I would have to move from overtop Margaret to allow the two of us to continue. Moving would expose the blood from the wound to Billy once again. I wasn't sure how he would react. I compliantly did as he instructed. I slowly lifted my body while staring at his stoic face. Billy was no longer looking at me. He had moved his eyes to Margaret. His expression did not change as her body came into view. He just stared quietly at the blood-drenched dress.

I took his hand to divert his attention even though he appeared at-ease with the situation. "Go. Climb up that cavern." I pointed over to the shaft that led to the well at the Commune. It was a reluctant request to get him away from her body. He would be closer to the evil that walks above us then he had ever been in his life. "At the top, before the opening, you will find an overcoat. Bring it back so we can use it as a wrap for Margaret's body." He nodded dutifully and swiftly made his way across the Sanctuary.

The overcoat had protected my clothes for years as I traveled up and down the tunnel to and from the Commune. Its services were no longer needed. I would never have to step foot in the Commune again. Never have to worry about missing a stain on my clothes that would lead to a beating, or worse, the discovery of the place that protected my son.

It seemed like just seconds for him to return with the coat in hand. I retrieved it from him and began to gently place it on Margaret. Billy kneeled beside me and would lift her arm or waist when needed to place the coat over her clothes. I tied the rope around her legs, waist and chest to keep it secured as we attempted to move her.

I paused and looked up at Billy. "I don't know where to take her?" I wasn't sure why I was asking Billy. How could he possibly know what to do in this situation. He hasn't even witnessed someone dying before.

Billy softly responded, "my ode woom." His pronunciation would intermittently relapse to when he was much younger.

It was perfect. It meant so much to me and would now be the best resting place for Margaret's body. I knew her soul was already being welcomed into a better place. Even though she took a life, I cannot imagine a God that would not forgive her actions. "Thank you, Billy." The room was far enough down the cave system that finding it would be challenging. Even if someone discovered the Sanctuary, if we removed the evidence, there would be no reason to explore the caves further.

Billy made his way to Margaret's shoulder. He wrapped his disfigured hands under her arms and with very little effort raised her off the ground. I was amazed at the strength he had given his small frame. Only Margaret's feet were now resting on the ground. Billy nodded for me to move.

It was much easier for me to lift the little bit of weight left. We worked as a team as we walked her body into the dark cavern. I had never entered the cavern without a torch. I trusted Billy's movements to guide us successfully to his boyhood room.

Billy began singing one of the nursery rhymes I sang to him when he was a child. I made up most of them. I wanted the words to fit the reality of what his childhood was like and not the perfect world depicted in many of the songs. His soft vocals replaced the silence in the underground cavern.

"Billy was a lit'el boy, lit'el boy, lit'el boy. Billy was a lit'el boy and soon he will gwowe. And Billy can go anywherwa, anywherwe in his cassel down ba'low." Hearing him reminded me of how sheltered he was from the real world. His pronunciation sounded just like it did when he was a toddler. We would sing the same song over and over when he was little. Each time we would increase the tempo. We always finished falling into each other and rolling on the ground in laughter. I am sure he was trying to comfort me but there was little joy in his words. The fear in his voice could be heard with every note as he continued singing the song. "Do not fallwo mawmee today, mawmee today, mawmee today. Do not fallwo mawmee today, it gowes aginst the wools." He was in an adult body and closer now to the size of a grown person, but his mind was still that of a child. I tried to do everything I could for him. And yet, I worry how he will interact with others when that day inevitably comes. His rage had intensified quickly when challenged by Jeremiah. His lack of understanding of the situation resulted in him attacking Margaret. The realization caused a tear to fall from my eye. Billy finished the last verse, "the two of us can waff and pway, waff and pway, waff and pway. The two of us can waff and pway, all others will be cruel." He articulated the last word perfectly.

I could sense he wanted me to join him as he hesitated before restarting the song. It didn't feel right as we slowly walked Margaret to his old room. Billy went on singing nervously without me accompanying him. He increased the volume each time he repeated the lyrics. It was just another way for him to encourage me to join. The third time around I could sense some anger in the sharpness of his tone. I reluctantly began to sing softly to ease his pain.

We made it to the entrance of his childhood room. We delicately placed Margaret inside. Billy fetched a torch and some matches for me to light the space. I found a knapsack to use to pack the remaining items that could trace someone to Billy. I collected several of the journals we had filled with words and pictures from the early years. Billy seemed uninterested in any of them. He just stood at the entrance and watched me clear the room. As I turned to leave, it dawned on me that I should say something out of respect for Margaret.

I returned to her side and knelt beside her. I placed my hand on her chest to cover her heart. A few biblical scriptures came to mind that were appropriate to honor her life. I felt disingenuous reciting them. I chose a different message. "Margaret, we are kindred spirits. Each of us found our way to the Commune without trying. Each of us imprisoned there until yesterday." A significant number of tears were now flowing from my eyes as I fought the fluids back from escaping my nose. "I have tried to believe in God. Belief in something bigger than all of this. I like to think there is a reward for doing what is right and consequences for harming others. I am not sure I believe that though. But you did. Through it all, your faith grew, and it inspired me to keep going. So maybe, maybe you were my angel. Sent to me for a reason. Either way, what I believe doesn't matter. What I know is you are a good person. You have a good soul. And you should be at peace having led the life you lived." I lowered myself over her to give her one last embrace.

Turning to leave, I saw a look of confusion on Billy's face. I brought the torch closer to him, "what is it Billy?"

The look on his face turned from one of confusion to fear. "Am I, good person?" He said it sheepishly as his chin dropped to his chest.

"Look at me, Billy. Look at me, son." His head lifted slowly as our eyes connected. I placed my free hand on his cheek. "You did not mean to harm Margaret.

You must want to hurt someone, hurt them for no other reason than to cause pain to be a bad person."

Billy's expression did not change. The fear could still be seen in his eyes. "Not her. The others."

My hand dropped from his face as I instinctively took a step back. The flames moving to and from causing shadows to dance across his face. As his mom, I didn't want to ask another question. I was afraid of what I might hear. Did I not teach him to be a good person? Did I not teach him to never hurt another person? I began to cry again as I implored him hoping he would answer positively. "Others? Billy? Have you hurt someone else?" I covered my mouth with the same hand that just seconds ago was caressing his face.

Billy's head dropped again as if it needed my hand for support to hold its position. I was staring directly at the two boney protrusions jetting out from his head. "I kill Lauwa's mawmee."

I fell against the rock surface below me. Laura. I haven't thought of her in years. I was exasperated. "Laura? Your friend from the woods? Why?" I pleaded for some rationale that would justify his actions.

Billy's head lifted again. This time his expression changed. The same rage I saw in his face when he was confronted by Jeremiah. "She beat Lauwa. Make Lauwa go way."

Wait. I remember. I remember the day I met Laura in the woods. The day Billy introduced me to her. The only time I talked to her. She had the wounds from her mothers' hands. It was the day we made the pact for the two of them to look out for one another. Just like with me, Billy was protecting her. How can I blame my child when he does not have the capacity to see beyond what is black and white? He was the product of the cold environment in which he was raised. As much as I tried to rationalize my efforts to nurture him, I had let him down. It was clear to me now. I am to blame for his jaded view of the world. I made the choice to keep him underground for so long. "Billy, it's not your fault. When did this happen?"

Billy's head shook from side to side as if he didn't know for sure. He struggled to get the words out as he began to get choked up thinking about it. "Long time…"

I replaced my hand on his cheek. His expression changed again. This time to a slight smile. He seemed like a burden he carried for years was finally lifted from his shoulders. For a moment, I wanted to reach out to hug him for all he has been through.

He said others. His language is not perfect. It could have been an easy mistake on his part or maybe I just heard him wrong. I hesitantly asked him to clarify his answer from before. "Did you mean others or just Laura's mom?"

This time the slight smile did not stray from his face. Out of the corner of his mouth, came the most terrifying of answers. "Others." He said it as clearly as the word cruel from the made-up nursery rhyme. I saw something different in him. Something I had never seen before. Or maybe, I just chose not to see it until now. I shuffled back several feet this time bumping into Margaret's body. I felt light-headed as my back landed across her legs. The strength to hold the torch upright was quickly dissipating. I heard Billy moving towards me. My eyes flickered several times before re-opening. He was now standing over me. The torch dropped behind me as everything turned to black.

Chapter 10: The Hunt Commences

"Jack Conway." I seldom received phone calls these days. Oh, there was a wrong number now and then and the occasional annoying sales pitch for unwanted items. Never any calls from someone I actually knew. I didn't mind though. I preferred the tranquil setting my life choices afforded me.

"Jack. Glad I caught you." I chuckled to myself knowing his chances were pretty good. "Chris Wagner."

The Sheriff. We had an up and down relationship over the past few years. I tried my best to transition the responsibilities in a manner reflective of the office we both held. One case continued to strain our relationship. Laura Perry's. It stuck with both of us before and after I retired. Sheriff Wagner even called me back a time or two, but it always went south. Often the result of me pushing for more resources dedicated to the investigation. I knew it was personal for me. I never understood why it didn't mean more to the rest of the community. "Sheriff." I paused genuinely surprised by the call. "To what do I owe this honor?" There may have been a mild sarcastic tone in my voice.

After an audible sigh he continued, "We have a situation. One I need your help on."

I was moving from surprise to a state of shock. I had been out of the game for some time. Sure, I continued my own investigation into Laura's disappearance, but without the badge I hit dead ends at almost every turn. "You want to run that by me again?"

Another sigh escaped before he continued. It was evident he did not want to make this call. His reticence piqued my interest even more. "I would rather go over this in person. Can you come by the station?"

I wasn't much for lying about my availability. There were exactly zero items on my schedule. Even still, I paused as if to suggest I was reviewing my calendar. "I think I can make that work."

Sheriff Wagner seemed irritated by the conversation with his quick retort, "Today, Jack. Need to see you today."

This must be important. A call out of the blue from a person that has been more of an adversary than a friend. The urgency of the timing. This was serious. I knew this tone from all the years I served. My demeanor changed instantly. My only thought was of the girl that I had searched for the past four years. "Is it Laura?" It sure sounded like the call. The call you never want to make as the Sheriff and, more significantly, the call you never want to receive from a Sheriff.

A longer than normal pause ensued before his response. Each second causing my nerves to raise ten-fold. "Jack. Can you just get down here as soon as you can?"

Deflection. He's avoiding the conversation. My mind was all over the place. Laura's mom, Jean. I was already jumping in my head to Jean. How would I tell her? "Sheriff Wagner, I'll come down to the station. I'll do it as soon as I get off this phone. I've been in your shoes. I have made these calls. I understand. You must answer me now. Is this...", It became more difficult to finish the sentence, "...regarding Laura Perry?"

"Jack. You know I think you are too close to that case to be any good. No. It is not about Laura Perry. Now will you get your ass down here so I can tell you what it is about?" He stressed the curse word while making his demand.

It was a weird feeling. At first relieved they had not found her body. I expected that call every day for the past four years. Each day that passed, reduced the odds of finding her alive. I knew it. And yet, the unknown has equally weighed on my mind. I know what it has done to Jean. It has been debilitating. She is barely a shell of the woman I knew before all this happened. "Thank you, Sheriff, for breaking protocol." I appreciated the honest answer. "I'll be there at 0900."

I hung up the phone and quickly gathered my things. The reality is I had been up since 5am. As much as I forced myself to sleep in, the early morning military routine still guided my internal clock. Some things cannot be undone. Before rushing off, I spent a minute or two retrieving a few case files. He said it had nothing to do with Laura Perry. I didn't believe him. Why else would he call me? It was the only major case that was still open from my tenure. And trust me, it haunts me daily.

I hopped in my pickup truck and turned it over. The engine fired up the same as the day I bought it. The truck rarely moved from the driveway most days. It had less than 10,000 miles even though I've had it for three years. Its use relegated to infrequent trips to the grocery and hardware stores. It doesn't take much to supply the rations for one individual. The farthest journey is when I visited Jean at the Senior Center. Even then it was only a 25-mile round trip. I used to take it out daily when I searched the woods. The trestles where Laura went missing were just a few miles from the house. I hadn't searched in a while though. I halted them after too many disappointments and the lack of new evidence to give me any confidence she would ever be found.

My random thoughts, combined with the speed at which I raced through town, passed the time quickly as I arrived within minutes to the station. The town wasn't much more than five or six blocks of densely placed buildings. It contrasted dramatically with the openness of everything else in the county.

I sat in the truck for a moment to avoid arriving too early. I still wasn't sure why Sheriff Wagner called for a meeting so early in the morning. I didn't want to appear too anxious as it might give my hand away. This is an emotion I fought my entire life. The men in my command would grow weary anytime units were asked to volunteer for missions. They knew it was not in me to decline the challenge but even more so to conceal my excitement. I always wanted to do more. Even now, at my age, I desired to have a sense of purpose again.

I walked up to the unassuming entrance of the Shelby County Sheriff's Office. It might as well be a law office or barber shop based on its appearance. Entering the office was something I had done countless times before. I opened the door causing the two bells that hung above it to clang together. The noise caused one of the two deputies in the room to acknowledge my presence.

"Sheriff Conway, welcome back." Deputy Tucker served under me for almost fifteen years before I retired in 1990. He extended his hand and a warm smile as I approached.

"Deputy Tucker. Still fighting crime in the metropolis of Shelby County." We both laughed knowing many of our calls required more of a babysitter than a police officer. Neither one of us minded though. Gary fought in Vietnam. I fought in World War II. We both had seen enough action to last a lifetime. I think our shared military history is what allowed us to work so well together. "How's the family?"

"The reason I'm still fighting crime!" I somewhat adopted Gary's family as mine when he served. I watched him raise his three children. I live vicariously through them. He sacrificed much for them as he did for our community and the country. He eventually got to answering the question. "All good. All growing up so fast. Scotty is in college. Can you believe that, college?"

I couldn't. I remember him riding in the cruiser too short to see over the bench seat. It didn't seem all that long ago. "That makes me really old Tucker."

"You are sir." He said it with a wry smile spreading across his face.

"You two love birds going to keep flirting or are we going to get to business?" The other Deputy in the office had stood up to announce his presence.

He was young. I am guessing in his mid-twenties. Sheriff Wagner hired him after I retired.

Deputy Tucker winked at me out of view of his fellow officer. "Jack, let me introduce you to the boy wonder. This here is Deputy Steven Curtis. Hired on straight out of college. He went to school for this stuff. Learned how to police in a classroom."

It was apparent the two of them did not have the same relationship as the two of us shared. Deputy Curtis responded aggressively, "I respect my elders, but anytime you want to see who can police better, you just let me know old man."

Deputy Tucker completely dismissed the naïve response from his colleague. The two of us went back to small talk leaving Curtis standing awkwardly in the middle of the room. He began to shuffle papers around to justify having stood up given our lack of reaction to his comment.

Another voice interrupted the two of us. Sheriff Wagner had stuck his head outside of the only private office in the room. "Jack. In here. Curtis you too."

I shook Deputy Tucker's hand one more time before making my way to the office I had served in for more than 20 years. As I entered, Sheriff Wagner motioned for me to sit. It always felt odd to be on this side of the desk. Deputy Curtis stood at the door still looking agitated by the earlier conversation. We were successful in getting him riled up.

I sat patiently as the Sheriff opened a case file and flipped through the documents. I took the time to look around to see what if anything had changed. Sheriff Wagner had a family so there were the obligatory family photos that never adorned my office. The only photos I had displayed were those with men I served in the military. The office was in disarray from my standards, but I realize I have high standards in this regard.

Sheriff Wagner spoke bringing my eyes back to him. "We have a report of a missing person." This wasn't the typical small-town case. I leaned in demonstrating my interest level.

Before Sheriff Wagner continued, he was interrupted by Curtis. "Sir, is this necessary? Why do we need his help?"

It was not hard to discern from the Sheriff's face the disdain he had for being interrupted. After a brief stare down of his young Deputy, he returned to address me. "Jeremiah Turner is considered a missing person. We received a report yesterday from his brother, Simon. We have reason to believe it is a legitimate missing persons case."

I leaned in even more. The Turner's have always been a polarizing family in the community. The patriarch, James, was universally adored up until his untimely death. The three sons operated in much different style. They isolated themselves and their few followers and restricted access to everyone else. James wanted everyone to be a part of his church. Under the new regime, it seemed to be by invitation only. Even as Sheriff, I only stepped on the property one time for the baptism of Simon's son. "Evidence?" I was intrigued enough to hear more.

Unbelievably, Deputy Curtis interrupted his superior officer once again. "Sir. This civilian…" He stressed the word before continuing, "has no right to learn the details of this case."

I commend him for his conviction while I waited for the Sheriff's response.

This time the stare transitioned to a brief but warranted verbal assault. "Curtis, you are here to keep your mouth shut. We covered this prior to this meeting. You do not have to be here. In fact, you do not have to be in the entire building. Or the county for that matter. Now shut the hell up!"

He had it coming. The Sheriff was still convulsing from the exchange when I attempted to get his attention. "Sheriff, the evidence?"

It took him a second to refocus on the question. "Forgive me, the evidence. There has been no sight of him for 48 hours. Jeremiah's truck is still in the same place. No other vehicles have left the premises. None of his personal items have been removed."

I followed the Sheriff's last statement building on the theory he was proposing. "So, he wasn't planning on going anywhere."

The Sheriff nodded. "According to Simon, the only thing missing is his shotgun."

I sat back in the chair contemplating what the Sheriff had expressed. I leaned back in before speaking, "Why am I here Sheriff?"

Deputy Curtis didn't speak but made a gesture as if to agree with my question. He was learning on the job.

Sheriff Wagner paused before answering. "Two reasons. One, we don't have the man- power for a missing persons case."

"And?" Again. prompting him to continue.

"Simon asked for you specifically." This time he leaned back in his chair.

I was taken aback by the answer. Why would he want me? The Sheriff could see the skeptical look on my face.

"Curtis, your're dismissed." The Sheriff wanted the room cleared for whatever he had to say. The Deputy moved slowly still disapproving of the whole meeting.

The door shut silencing every noise from outside the small office. The Sheriff stood up and walked past me. He made his way to the only window that looked out over the rest of the station. His back to me, he began to draw the blinds obscuring the view. My head followed his footsteps back to the desk. He slowly opened the metal desk drawer. A high-pitched screech accompanied the movement. Mercifully, it came to a stop. The Sheriff retrieved a file and placed it on the desk between the two of us. I didn't need him to tell me what it contained. The cover was worn and tattered from all the nights I had handled it. It was the one file I had left for him in the desk. The rest I had returned to the storage room.

He opened the file and removed a single sheet of paper. He presented it to me by sliding it across the desk. He tapped his finger on the top edge several times before speaking. "You drew this didn't you?"

He was referring to the map of the Commune I had sketched some thirty years ago. "Yes."

His hand pulled back as he relaxed his outstretched arm. "Why?"

I knew where he was going with the whole line of questioning. I employed the same tactics many times. Keep your questions vague. Don't give away too much. Silence is the best way to get someone to talk. Let the person on the other side of the desk fill the space with the details that could uncover what you need. I shrugged off the question without saying a word. As if to imply the map had little importance. The Sheriff stood up again and moved towards me. He leaned to the side to support his weight on the edge of the desk. He was now just a few feet from where I sat. Did he really think he could intimidate me? I remained silent.

An awkward amount of time passed while we both tried to upstage one another. The Sheriff gave in. "Oh Jack, we don't have time for a pissing match." He transitioned from the stern look he held to a more friendly disposition. "C'mon. The only way I can have you help with this case, is if you give me a reason. Give me something that shows you can break through the fortress that is the Divine Commune."

It was a valid point. And, I really wanted in. I nodded. Sheriff Wagner returned to his chair as I picked up the map to view it more closely. "My predecessor made me aware of some irregularities involving how James Turner died. He had no proof, but he was convinced it was no accident. Where is the note?" I did not see the evidence bag among the items in the file.

The Sheriff acted as if he didn't hear what I asked. I continued to stare at him prompting a response. "Excuse me?"

Back to playing the game. I decided to call his bluff. "Sheriff, if you want my help, you are going to have to share everything you know about this case. Either that or I go back to enjoying the view from my deck."

He didn't like being backed into a corner, but I somehow had enough leverage given his desire to the resolve the case quickly. He acquiesced with a subtle nod of his head. He opened the top drawer in his desk and retrieved the evidence bag containing the blood- stained note.

"That note was written by James Turner. It is his blood covering the paper. Just before James died, he handed it to my predecessor. It was my first day on the job. The day the retiring Sheriff shared the incident with me. From what gathered, James feared what his sons might do. That is why he had taken the time to put on paper his final words. Those words have only been seen by four people, two of which are now dead."

The Sheriff began shaking his head side to side. I did not know what to make of his reaction. "I've heard those rumors for years. What does that have to do today with Jeremiah? And, why have they asked for you?" I had no answer for why Simon would ask for me after all these years.

"I remember walking the grounds of the Divine Commune like it was yesterday. Simon had invited me to his son's baptism. I made note of every detail, every structure, every individual I met." I paused before continuing, "I met one person that stood out from the crowd."

The Sheriff was now all in. Edge of his seat with his fingers clasping the front of his desk. "Go on."

I exhaled, "her name was Margaret. At the time of my visit, she had been married to Jeremiah for about a year. She was with child. I could sense something was off in the immediate exchange I had with her. She sought me out after the service. Margaret was doing her best to tell me something important. Something that was bothering her. Unfortunately, Simon interrupted our conversation and sent Margaret away."

"So, what!" The Sheriff was growing more and more impatient with me.

I had one chance to sell him on how I could help resolve the case. "I connected with Margaret. She was going to talk to me. I know it. I think she will talk to me again. I believe she is the key to uncovering all that has happened behind those walls.

The Sheriff shook his head as if he couldn't believe what he was about to say. "Simon trusts you. He knows you know the woods. He knows you know the families involved. Not to mention, Curtis stepped all over himself yesterday while responding to the report at the Divine Commune." The Sheriff rolled his eyes at the incompetence of his young Deputy.

I sat back to digest what was being requested. I knew my answer. There was no way I wouldn't help with the case. I have wanted to search the Commune ever since Laura went missing. It was the only area a judge would not grant a search warrant. I could care less about Jeremiah. He is just a means to an end. I had one final request before I would take this on. I needed to have full police authority. "Sheriff, I will need to be sworn in. I'll need the badge."

The Sheriff nodded to confirm my request.

My search for Laura resurrected.

Chapter 11: Peacekeeper

I opened the door of the office with the badge pinned to my coat. I made sure Deputy Curtis could see it as I passed by his desk. Sheriff Wagner was now standing in his doorway as I made my way over to the cabinet that housed the firearms.

Officer Tucker met me with the key in hand. He gave me a warm smile before leaning in to whisper in my ear, "You sure about this?"

I returned the favor by leaning over to whisper in his ear, "I'm too old to hear a whisper." Pulling away, I smiled back at him as he placed the key in my hand. We both turned to look at Deputy Curtis, who as much as he tried, was attempting to act like he wasn't watching.

I opened the cabinet to see a much different arsenal than what I remembered. Deputy Tucker could sense I had no idea which gun to select.

"Jack, you're going to want this one. It's a 9mm Glock 19. Latest thing on the market to make sure we have the edge on the bad guys. Trust me, it will keep the peace." He gently handed the firearm to me.

I've held more weapons in my hands than I cared to over the past 50 years, but nothing felt like this. "This doesn't feel like my .357."

"You might want to practice with that thing first before you get out there in the field." Gary winked at me as he handed me a case of the magazines. "Twelve bullets in each round. Even if you miss with the first ten, you can still get shots eleven and twelve off within a total of ten seconds."

If only we had this fire power in Peleliu. "You might need twelve shots Tucker, I only ever needed one!" The playful teasing was a necessity in a job where your life could be put in peril at any moment. "Explains why you sit behind a desk now!"

I knew a retort of some kind was coming, "Just don't shoot that from your rocking chair Jack, you'll flip right off the back of the damn thing."

I guess Deputy Curtis had heard enough. He stood up and walked out muttering a few words under his breath. "I'm getting lunch before you dinosaurs accidently shoot me."

Gary couldn't resist getting in one more jab, "If we're old than why are you the one getting lunch at 10:45am." Curtis looked stumped as he glanced at his wristwatch. Failing to come up with a response, he exited with a louder than needed shutting of the door.

The two of us started laughing out loud. Sheriff Wagner joined in now that the deputy had left the office.

"Jack let me walk you out." The Sheriff waved his arm motioning toward the door.

I shook Gary's hand one more time before following the Sheriff out of the office.

Walking side by side the Sheriff recapped the goals of the case. "Build on the trust Simon feels for you. You must get access to Margaret. She may hold the key to finding out what happened to Jeremiah. The only way Simon lets one of his sheep talk is if he trusts you. Who knows what else goes on behind those walls? It will be a tight-rope Jack. You have to stay focused on Jeremiah or Simon will shut us out."

The message was clear to me. I was being given some latitude, even if it came with a warning. "Yes, sir."

The Sheriff stopped in his tracks just before we reached my truck. He slapped the case file on the Turner's against my chest. "I have to ask Jack."

"Sir?" I played it cool even though I had a hunch as to where this was headed.

"The girl has nothing to do with this. You need to be focused on this case." He tapped the file against my chest again.

I didn't respond. There was really nothing I could say. He was right. Laura does distract me from most everything I do. My silence was enough to justify his concern.

"Jack, I mean it. Simon will see right through it." I nodded before he finished his thought. "And she's gone Jack. You know it. You know the time that has passed. You know the statistics. The probability of her still being out there somewhere and surviving on her own our miniscule."

I did not agree at all with the rest of his statement. I never have and never will until I have proof. It is the reason the Sheriff pulled me from assisting on Laura's case a few years ago. I know the odds are against finding her alive, but I owe it to her mom to provide closure one way or another. I said nothing.

The lack of a response irritated the Sheriff. "I am going to send you out there. Send you out with the authority of this office." He collected himself before continuing. "If I hear or become aware of anything you do that jeopardizes this case, I will pull those privileges just as quickly as I gave them to you today." His teeth smashed together at the end his words causing even more bass to be heard in his tone. He knew I had the upper hand and it was killing him. "Simon is expecting you at the Commune today."

I plucked the folder he had pinned against my chest leaving his raised hand empty. This power struggle had gone on too long. "Sir, I know what I am being asked to do. I am grateful you have reached out to me to do it. I will do everything in my power to find out what happened to Jeremiah Turner." What I didn't say is Laura will always be my priority. The Sheriff could say anything, and it wouldn't change my feelings.

"Wait." The Sheriff walked to his patrol car and popped the trunk. He retrieved a two-way radio from the vehicle. "I want you to give regular reports. Updates at least twice a day and any other time you discover anything meaningful." He handed over the small box and cables. I balanced everything including the case file awkwardly in my arms.

I stepped away half expecting him to stop me. He didn't. I placed the case file under the passenger seat while climbing behind the steering wheel. I temporarily stashed the Glock in the glove compartment and placed the magazines beside me. Untangling the cords of the radio, I inserted the charger into the cigarette lighter. A small light on the side of the microphone flashed. Pushing the talk button, I tested the communication tool, "regular reports, over." The patrol car was close enough for me to hear an echo of my words transmitted through the sheriff's radio.

The Sheriff's arms folded over one another in front of his chest. As I pulled back from the parking spot the Sheriff yelled out over the noise of my truck's engine, "REGULAR REPORTS!"

I decided to heed the advice of Deputy Tucker. It had been a while since I fired a gun and nothing as powerful as the weapon he recommended. I drove home to get acclimated to my new side piece.

I had enough land to safely discharge a firearm on my property. The makeshift firing range at the back of my lot supported many years of target practice. It kept my skills strong while I still was serving as Sheriff. I could shoot at ranges of up to 100 yards with any errant shots collected by the ten-foot-high wall of dirt I built as a backstop.

I placed three targets on hay bales about twenty feet from the mound of dirt. The paper targets were silhouettes of a human-being. I preferred the bullseye targets as shooting at another human is nothing that I relish doing. It was, however, a necessity to protect others or even myself while in the field. I paced off 30 yards and took aim at the first target.

I fired off four quick shots aiming two to the chest and two to the head of the first target. Hay went flying from behind the target on three of the shots. The power contained in this pistol was magnificent. The engineering alone was something to behold. I turned and paced off another 30 yards. I rattled off four more shots at the second target.

Once again, I retreated 30 yards for my final four shots. I took aim at the silhouette. I imagined a man holding Laura captive. He had her pinned against his side with his own firearm touching her head. I had one chance to save her life. I had to be accurate. I could easily hit her or give him time to fire if I missed my mark. The target was stationary. Real life targets are almost always moving. I took small steps side to side to simulate firing under these conditions. The movement combined with the squinting of my eyes caused the silhouette to dance around in a shadowy blur. I sent four more shots in quick succession. It was so rapid it seemed each bullet would push the other while flying on their way to the target.

I holstered the Glock and began marching toward the targets to inspect the results. I approached the 30-yard target first. I traced my finger over the location where each bullet entered. The size of each hole was much larger than what my .357 could produce. Three holes. I must have missed with one of my shots. It was clear I was rusty and not as precise with this new weapon. The shots would have downed the subject but not as quickly as is needed to save lives.

I moved to the second target. All four bullets struck the target with three landing inside the confines of the silhouette. Good, but not great. If this were basic training, I would be running for hours for my lack of accuracy.

I walked over to the final target. There was only one hole. It was located between the eyes of the blackened silhouette. However, it was much larger. Two times the size of the previous targets. Multiple bullets had entered and exited through roughly the same space. Thinking of Laura intensified my focus on the target. I smiled knowing the shots would have instantly downed the individual. Laura would have been unscathed and free of her captor. The accuracy boosted my confidence. I can bring her home.

Chapter 12: The Sermon

I opened the closet to reveal numerous hangers with clothes dangling from each of them. I didn't have much need to open the closet nowadays. Most of the clothing I needed came from the chest of drawers. It was another benefit of retired life. I pulled a handful of clothes to the left. The hangers screeched across the metal rod supporting the outfits. They squeezed together on one side of the closet. This left four items hanging to my right. Two officer uniforms were pressed and hanging neatly encased in a plastic see through wrap. Behind them, were two of my dress blues from my military days. I ran my hand over the shoulder of the military garb. It was decorated with various medals from the time I served our country.

The Sheriff uniform was plain by contrast. Even the beige coloring was bland compared to the vibrant color of the military uniforms. I lifted the officer clothes off the rack and placed them on my bed. I had no doubt it would still fit. I worked hard to maintain my physique. If I fell short of finding and rescuing Laura, it was not going to be a result of my lack of conditioning.

I got dressed and looked in the mirror. I straightened my collar and repositioned my belt line. I could still pass inspection, I thought to myself. I found it important in my civil service to keep appearances. It helped in many ways. Witnesses were more likely to be truthful, criminals more easily subdued, and some individuals so intimidated they would avoid crime altogether. It wasn't the same in war. In fact, the dress often made you a larger target. The more decorations adorning your uniform, the more bullets sent your way.

Dressed and armed, I made my way to my truck to drive to the Commune. It was time to launch the investigation.

I recognized a nervous energy as I drove the familiar roads. It was a feeling I hadn't felt in some time. It reminded me of my first few days on the job many years ago. I kind of liked the feeling. For a guy my age, it was a welcome change. The woods to my left were dense due to the remaining summer foliage. It wasn't until I was right on top of it that the trestles came into view at my nine o' clock. It made my return real. The nervous energy now replaced with an ache deep in my gut. The flashes of the trestle through the leaves were interwoven with the faces of the young people I had met. Their expressions filled with pain, or in a few cases, the cold look of mortality. Luke's childlike face lingered longer in my mind as he was the first to have fallen at the trestle. He was also the youngest. Only ten when the train threw him from a height too high to survive. He was the reason I met Laura. She somehow lived through the ordeal. I wish that event would have ended the list of victims. Unfortunately, it has continued all these years. Each victim contributing to the urban legend of a mythical creature. An entity that lures young people out onto the trestle. As outrageous as that sounds, I know this to be true. Evil resides in and around the woods. There's far too much evidence to come to any other conclusion.

The thoughts almost caused me to miss the left turn to the Divine Commune. I pulled off the main road and slowly drove down the rocky, dirt path. Everything looked exactly like the last time I was on this road. The only difference is the thicker concentration of trees now creating a canopy over the property. Foot off the gas, I idled my way forward to the entrance gate. The last time I was here I was greeted by a young lady. I would later come to find out it was Margaret, Jeremiah's wife. She was dressed properly like a Puritan. I can still see her half smile and forced wave as I approach the gate.

Today, there was no one waiting for me. It dawned on me that I was not given an exact time to arrive. They did not expect me. Would they still welcome me?

I eased my truck to a slow stop a few feet in front of the gate. My fingers tapping on the top of the steering wheel. I leaned in to see if I could make anything out through the cracks in the wooden barrier. Squinting my eyes to focus my vision on any movement from behind the wall. My back alerted me of the awkward position I had maintained after several minutes. I figured waiting to be invited in was the best course of action. The last thing I wanted to do was pull a Curtis and be removed from the case.

I returned my shoulders against the upholstery of the vehicle keeping a close watch on my surroundings. I saw flashes of something moving inside the fence line. The height of the wall kept me from seeing anything above it's reaches. Whatever it was, it was moving swiftly. I lowered the driver's side window a quarter of the way down. The sound was unmistakable. The galloping noise of a horse was closing in on my location. Collect yourself. Maintain your composure. Do not mess this opportunity up. I took several deep breaths. My presence outside the gate was detected much faster than seemed possible.

The noise from the horse subsided as the rider dismounted. I could not make out the person heading to the gate. I moved my right hand from the steering wheel to my thigh. It was now just a few inches from the Glock resting against my hip. The gate began to open after the chain was unlocked and removed. Simon himself had come to greet me. He opened the two swinging sections wide enough for my truck to pass through. He motioned for me to drive in. I lifted my foot off the brake and began to idle forward. I came within inches of Simon as I passed by him.

The look of concern was easy to see in his appearance. A face that looked to have aged much faster than the years that had passed since I last saw him. His thin body type enhanced the skeletal look of his eyes and cheek bones. He rarely left the Commune these days and from the color of his skin spent most of his time shielded from the sun.

I watched through my rearview mirror as Simon secured the gate behind me. He walked his horse alongside the truck as I lowered the window the rest of the way.

"Reverend." I nodded my head as I acknowledged his approach.

He did not respond immediately. It seemed evident he was trying to find the right words and control his emotions. We both had this in common but for very different reasons. The Turner family was close. They grew up together. All three brothers within a stone's throw of one another their entire life.

His lips smacked together a couple of times to remove the saliva that had collected in his mouth. "I'm glad you came, Sheriff." He looked away off into the distance. "I prayed you would come and help us through this difficult time and here you are. God is good." He looked back to me and did his best to force a smile.

I nodded and left the last statement he made go unanswered. "It's just Jack now. I've been deputized to help but it's just Jack."

Simon looked surprised by my words and even a little irritated. "No. No, sir. You will always be my Sheriff. You kept your word all those years. You kept the community around us safe and you let the Divine Commune serve God in our own way. You allowed God's law to rein sovereign inside these walls." He tapped the side of the truck to emphasize the point.

His response shocked me more than my dismissal of the title he continued to use. For a man of action, the thought that I had condoned whatever transpired here has been my greatest regret as the Sheriff. To hear him acknowledge it, made it even worse. It dawned on me that he was not only speaking to the past, but the present situation. It was a veiled threat, but nonetheless, an underlying message to tread lightly. He already had me cornered in the first few minutes of our exchange. Stick to his brother. Forget about the rest of it. "Jeremiah." I abruptly changed the direction the conversation was heading. "I was sorry to hear about his disappearance." The words were delivered with little emotion. Simon would easily detect the false concern if I tried to empathize and share in his grief.

The aggressive tone he had transitioned to switched back to one of helplessness. His reaction validated how I could maintain some control over the investigation. His head dropped this time as he fought back tears. His emotions distorted his words as he continued. "First. First, we go to church. You are just in time for a prayer service for Jeremiah and his family." His hand wiped across his face clearing any fluids that had made their way past his failed attempts to stop them. "We may have you Sheriff, but we will need God's strength and wisdom to find my brother."

I had little choice but to go along with his plan. If I objected, I would most likely be asked to leave until the service concluded. I knew he would not let me roam the property completely unsupervised. The service may also give me a chance to connect with Margaret. A prospect that made the invitation bearable. "Thank you for the invitation, Reverend."

Simon reached into the truck and sandwiched my hand between his and the steering wheel. He squeezed his fingers pressing my flesh into the leather covering. He looked up and spoke through cries and emotional outbursts. "My strength is dried up like a potsherd; and my tongue cleaveth to my jaws; and thou hast brought me into the dust of death." I closed my eyes hoping he would release my hand, but he continued preaching. "For my life is spent with grief, and my years with sighing: my strength faileth because of mine iniquity, and my bones consumed." Simon slammed his other hand on top of his putting even more pressure on the steering wheel. "With whom my hand shall be established: mine arm also shall strengthen him." He was now yelling the words as he continued. "For thou hast been a strength to the poor, a strength to the needy in his distress, a refuge from the storm, a shadow from the heat, when the blast of the terrible ones is as a storm."

Simon was breathing rapidly as he concluded his words. His head still down hidden by his outstretched arms. His grip relaxed freeing my hand of his painful clutch. He looked away as he slammed his hand against the side of my truck. I jumped to the right as the sound filled the space around me. He said nothing as he walked away. I watched him closely in the side view mirror still on edge from the last few minutes. He mounted the horse and trotted past me. He never looked back as he moved in front of my truck. He waved for me to follow. As if the episode was not disconcerting enough, I was now heading to his church. A place I remembered like yesterday.

I allowed the horse plenty of room before resuming the drive. The road was now more dirt than rock. The slow pace gave me ample time to see everything I passed in detail. On my left, I saw the circular configuration of benches from the original outdoor church. It is the place James Turner started it all nearly 80 years ago. It is also where I saw his aging wife repeatedly strike herself in the head on my last visit to the Commune. The image has never left my memory. The blood and bruising of her self-inflicted wounds still haunt me today. It has been 30 years since she stood on that pew and inexplicably beat herself.

Leaving the outdoor church behind, we entered a wooded section. The trees reached even higher to the sky and had widened as well. The path narrowed as the branches extended brushing the sides of my truck. Above me, the branches connected with the trees across the road creating a tunnel like passage.

Even though the sun had risen, the shade of the trees cast a dark shadow. The darkness enveloped Simon making it difficult to see his exact location. I flipped on the headlights to ensure I was keeping a safe distance from him and his horse. The beams of light extended far beyond him. It projected a shadow in front of him. The shadow exaggerated the movements of the mare. Jumping quickly side to side as the light caromed off the shifting motion of the horse. It was mesmerizing. Almost hypnotic as we continued down the darkened path.

The headlights faded into the natural light as we made it to the open field where the new church was located. I continued to follow Simon until I veered off to park in the designated area. I pulled in beside a few cars already positioned in the grassy field. It was apparent, by the lack of tracks in the dew-covered grass, that they had been there for some time. Perhaps they were friends of the church assisting with the search.

Before I exited the vehicle, I picked up the radio. "Sheriff Wagner, do you read me."

A great deal of feedback accompanied his response, "Yes, Deputy Conway. What is your status. Over."

I think I preferred Simon referencing me inappropriately as Sheriff over Wags condescending emphasis on the word Deputy. "I'm reporting. On location at the Divine Commune. Have made contact with Simon. Readying to attend a prayer service for Jeremiah. Over."

I released the talk button hoping for a quick response. The delay in leaving my truck was being noticed. The Sheriff was laughing as he replied, "church, they got you going to church."

My patience had worn thin with the conversation. I didn't like checking in to begin with but less so with frivolous banter. "I have to go. Over." I tossed the radio into the bench seat as the Sheriff retorted.

"Wait. Jack. Tell me…" I shut the door of my truck essentially ending the fruitless interchange. He knew where I was and what I was doing next. I consider that to be one of my two obligatory reports.

Walking to the church entrance, I saw Simon securing his mount to a post. There were several horses tethered to the same wooden structure. Another rider approached as Simon was finishing. He dismounted quickly and moved along side Simon. The two were talking and looking in my direction. I attempted to downplay my awareness of their actions by looking around the Commune. The Commune was breathtaking in its simplicity. Other than the cars, you felt transported back to an earlier time.

I made it to the church door and decided to take one more look in Simon's direction. This time the other person was pointing at me as they finished their conversation. I did not recall having seen him before. I entered the church without pausing to avoid appearing suspicious of their actions. Trust needed to be established and all eyes were on me. It was evident that I would be treated as an outsider.

Inside the church there were strikingly few people. A smattering spread out across the pews. Each of them taking turns looking in my direction before refocusing on the cross at the front of the church. No one was speaking. It was very solemn. I took a seat towards the back as I attempted to identify everyone.

Simon's family was the easiest. His wife was in the front pew with her now grown children by her side.

She leaned on the oldest child's shoulder and was visibly sobbing as she held a tissue to her face.

A few aisles back was another man that was close to Simon's age. I assume it was Elijah the middle brother in the Turner family. He had his arms around a woman of a similar age.

Two other families were in the pews between where I sat and the front of the church. Seventeen total people in all. No one under the age of 16. The last time I was here the church was filled with young children. The structure and the members had both aged.

A few minutes passed with no activity. It gave me a chance to take in the surroundings. The interior of the church had deteriorated significantly since my last visit. The seemingly declining number of followers represented in the lack of care given to the facility. The pews have been altered since my last visit. A single board added to provide some much-needed back support. It allowed the hymnals to be placed on the back of each board. The newer condition of the back support contrasted with the weathered look of the aged benches.

The doors to the church opened behind me and Simon walked in followed by four other men. I recognized none of them. They were all dressed for outdoor work and not a religious service.

The number of strangers reinforced Simon's words that I had neglected this place while I was the acting sheriff. It was going to be that much more difficult to build trust with people I have never met.

I caught myself. I glanced back around at every person that was now inside. How could I have overlooked the obvious. Margaret was not in the church. Her face was one I would not have forgotten. She may be in mourning but where better to do that than at this service. Especially given the passion the congregation has for expressing their spiritual beliefs.

Simon was now standing at the altar. Those that were still seated made it to their feet.

Simon began to speak to the congregation. His demeanor changed from a conflicted individual to a confident preacher. The years of routine kicked in masking the personal family distress that had consumed him.

"My fellow brothers and sisters, we are gathered here today to ask for his divine intervention. To provide us with the fortitude to find our lost sheep and bring him home." As Simon finished those around me shouted Amen. I was late to join in having been caught off guard by the quick response. This drew even more glances from the few people around me.

Simon retrieved a bible from the lectern and lifted it over his head. He placed it in front of him and removed the tassel of fabric that had marked a passage. His voice raised as he delivered the words. "Isaiah 63:6 – And I will tread down the people in my anger, and make them drunk in my fury, and I will bring down their strength to earth."

My head jumped from person to person as they shouted over each other, "Praise him, Amen, Alleluia..."

Simon closed the bible and expanded on the words in the passage. "You see my brothers and sisters, it is okay to be angry, it is okay to ask for the strength of our God to act when needed. God made each of us. He knows our limitations better than anyone. He knows the inherent struggle we have as humans to live a pure and just life. He knows there are times we will be tested. How will we respond?" Simon one by one made eye contact with everyone in the small congregation. "I believe, that is what God wants for us now. I believe he is testing our resolve. He is testing our faith."

More affirmations were shouted from the pews. Simon absorbed them all as he opened his arms to his followers.

The yelling ceased and Simon walked to the edge of the steps of the raised platform. Before he could speak another person from the church shouted out, "what about her?" He strained to get it out as he was overcome with emotion. He held on to the bench in front of him to keep from falling over. All eyes looked his way before returning to Simon. It was clear they wanted to hear his response.

Simon was taken off guard by the comment. He was clearly agitated by the interruption. "I adore you nephew. Now is not the time. We need our strength to find Jeremiah."

It must be Ezekiel, the oldest son of Jeremiah and Margaret. A young man raced over to brace him.

Simon diverted everyone's attention to the altar once again. "Now come forward each of you to receive the divine spirit. The spirit that will lead us to our lost sheep."

One by one each church member filed out and assembled at the front of the church. Even Ezekiel made his way with the help of the younger man by his side. I was now the only one left standing in a pew.

Simon looked towards me. "Sheriff, this prayer is meant for you. You are the vessel for his inspiration. Please come forward."

Was this really happening? I reluctantly complied as I shifted down the aisle to the main walkway. I approached the semi-circle the congregation had made on the stairs of the altar. Simon was positioned in the center with his arms wide nodding at me to continue moving towards him. The group started to hum as I made my way by each pew. It was growing louder and louder as I approached.

I attempted to divert off to one side, but Simon shook his head and lowered a hand in my direction. He wanted me to join him in the center. I took two more steps forward now flanked by members of the church on either side of me. They closed in behind creating a circle around me.

Simon took my hand and extended it over head. The humming continued. The closeness of the bodies made me extremely uncomfortable. I could not determine if any were a threat. I had little room to operate should the need arise to pull my sidearm.

Those around me extended an arm reaching towards Simon's hand. They pressed in closer as their fingers pressed against my outstretched arm. The humming persisted. It created a great deal of heat from the close-knit pack of human bodies.

Simon shouted over the humming, "the fool hath said in his heart, there is no God. They are corrupt, they have done abominable works." The humming was only dissected by shouts confirming the words spoken by Simon.

He was casting judgment on me. It was the only way he could reconcile asking me for help. He was baptizing me in his faith. He continued bellowing the words from his mouth, "strangers have devoured his strength, and he knoweth it not: yea, gray hairs are here and there upon him, yet he knoweth not."

I was feeling nauseous in such close quarters. This had to end soon, or I would be forced to fight my way out.

Simon's voice thundered again, "blessed be the LORD my strength, which teacheth my hands to war, and my fingers to fight. Give this man your strength and instill him with your faith." Simon looked to the ceiling of the church as the last few words left his mouth.

The individuals around me broke from humming and into a song. The words blended as my head swiveled from face-to-face. They were all singing loudly except one. Ezekiel was not singing. He stared at me while the others raised their heads to the ceiling.

He mouthed one name, "Margaret." A tear fell from his eye as he turned and ran out of the church. I wanted to follow him, but it would have been viewed as disrespectful by those around me. The song ended and each person let their hand run down my arm and over my body as they moved away. They proceeded out of the church leaving me at the alter with only Simon.

I fell to the steps and leaned back on my elbow.

"I can remember the first time I felt God's love. It can be overwhelming. We do not have the capacity as humans to fully embrace him." Simon sat beside me on the top step.

"Reverend, I need to investigate. Time in these cases is our greatest enemy." I participated in his ceremony and I hoped he would let me move on to what I am good at, policing.

Simon chuckled, a break from his somber disposition for most of the morning, "Sheriff, there is a far greater enemy facing all of us. It would do you well to embrace God's love and his guidance. Your dismissal of him weakens you and your chances of finding salvation. Finding the answers you seek."

I didn't have time for a philosophical debate. I feared this tug of war could go on for hours. Rather than respond, I allowed space for Simon to talk. If I challenged him this would go on forever.

The stoic demeanor returned. Simon responded with a collaborative tone, "what is it that you need, sheriff?"

We may finally be getting somewhere. The first two activities in any investigation are always the same. I have done this for 30 years and it is a tried and true method. "First, I need to talk to everyone, individually. Second, I need to inspect everything." It was a lot to ask, but it would test Simon's desire to answer the question of what happened to his brother.

Simon slowly nodded his head. "Of course, I trust you will do the right thing Sheriff." He paused before continuing, "especially now that you are filled with the wisdom of the holy spirit."

I let the last part go. I had what I needed. I stood up to start investigating before Simon stopped me again with a few more words.

"Elijah will be your guide. He will take you anywhere you want to go." His trust only went so far and maybe even the strength of his faith.

Chapter 13: Notes

Elijah was waiting for me as I exited the church. It was all planned. I felt like a pawn in their game. "Where to first Sheriff?" He tipped his hat from atop his horse.

Jack. I am not the Sheriff! It was no use saying it out loud. Everything in the Commune was 30 years behind the rest of the world. In that respect, I would have just started serving my term as Sheriff of Shelby County. It was apparent the Turner's preferred things to stay the same. "Jeremiah's home."

Elijah nodded, "figured you might say that. You ride? We'll get along must faster than by foot."

It had been awhile since I had been on a horse. I would have said no if not for the time it would save. "Sure. I've done some riding."

Elijah pointed to another horse hitched to a post on the side of the church. "You can ride Moses. He is one of our oldest, yet most reliable mares."

I internalized the laughter at the thought of riding a horse named Moses. "We should get along fine since we both have a lot of mileage." Here's to hoping he has mellowed and not given to becoming crankier with age. I'm not sure I could say that about myself.

Riding was going to be easier than mounting the beast. I was in my forties the last time I rode. The horse circled around as I attempted to push off the stirrup with my left leg and swing my body on to the saddle. Moses and I did a complete 360 before I landed on top of him. I smiled at Elijah now that I was safely perched atop the horse.

He kicked at the side of his mount and took off quickly from the stationary position.

I kicked at Moses and without fail he raced towards the other horse. My focus was on riding and following Elijah's lead. I noticed at least two weapons he had on his person. A shotgun was positioned at his side and a pistol was holstered on his hip. He was within his right to carry firearms on his property, but it took away another dimension of authority I usually held over those I investigated.

We arrived at a small cabin within minutes of leaving the church. I pulled up beside Elijah to hear further instructions.

"This is it. Jeremiah and Margaret have lived here for 30 years. They raised Ezekiel and Thomas, their two kids, in this house." He nodded towards the home as if to tell me to get going.

I more or less fell off the horse as Elijah reached over to steady Moses. It was hard to believe he was going to let me investigate unsupervised. I took a few steps before he spoke again. I figured it was too good to be true.

"Now Sheriff, you do your policing thing. And you bring my brother home." For the first time, I could hear his voice wavering from emotion. "I'll wait here for you."

Facing away from Elijah, I turned my head slightly and lowered my chin to my shoulder to acknowledge his request. He didn't want to slow me down. His actions also implied he was not involved with Jeremiah's disappearance. It's always the little things that connect the dots to form a picture. You just listen carefully, take notes, and almost always the answer becomes apparent.

I walked up to the cabin door and climbed the few steps to the entrance. I visually inspected the area to see if there were any signs of forced entry. There only appeared to be the normal wear and tear typical of a structure this old. I retrieved my note pad from my pocket and opened the door. Across the room, I saw Ezekiel on his knees with his fingers interlocked together in front of him. He was the only one in the cabin. I shut the door behind me. As much as Elijah didn't want to get in the way, I am sure he would be interested in whatever I might find. This knowledge could intentionally or unintentionally be shared with a potential person of interest, thus compromising the investigation.

I approached Ezekiel slowly as he seemed unaware that I had entered the room. I inspected every inch as I closed in on his location. He was softly mumbling words that were difficult to discern. I tapped him on his shoulder to bring him out of whatever trance like state he was in.

Ezekiel turned his head to me exposing the tears that were streaming down his face. He turned away from me and said, "Amen."

He had been praying. His hands stretched out over one of the four beds that occupied the small room. He brought them both down and used them to push himself up as he sat on the edge of the bed.

"It's Ezekiel?" I sought to confirm his identity.

He wiped the tears from his face with his sleeve and responded, "Yes sir."

I nodded and sat beside him on the bed. It made a sound like it was not used to carrying that much weight. "I'm going to get a chair." The exchange brought out a quick but welcomed smile from the conflicted young man.

I pulled a chair from the kitchen table over to Ezekiel.
I sat on it backwards and placed my arms on the top
of the back support. My pad was extended out in
front of me just a few inches from his face. "I see four
beds. Who all lived here?"

Ezekiel looked around as if to confirm no one else
was listening. He still seemed reticent to talk. This is
what I had encountered in almost every case I ever
investigated. People do not talk for a variety of
reasons. They may be intimidated, they may not
trust you, sometimes they are just shy or
confrontational, the list goes on and on. I think
Ezekiel was none of that. I think he is scared.

I reached out and put my left hand on his shoulder.
"It's okay son."

Before my hand left his shoulder, he began to speak.
"Mom and dad." He pointed to the largest bed over in
the corner of the room. "Christine." He pointed to a
bed on the far side of the cabin that was isolated from
the others.

I began scribbling the names on my pad.

"Thomas." His finger moved to another bed just a few
feet from where we sat. Both of his hands patted the
edge of the bed he was sitting on. Mine."

I asked the next question in a matter of fact way as not to convey any judgment. "How old are you Ezekiel?"

"Twenty-eight." He had a sad look on his face as if he was embarrassed by the admission.

I attempted again to comfort him by breaking from the more formal interview questions. It was a technique that I had to practice to master. I used to barrel through an interview. I discovered, after several early cases, I had rarely collected the information needed. I had become much more methodical interviewing people of interest. "I met you once Ezekiel."

His eyes widened and he looked confused. "I don't, remember, meeting you, sir." His response paced to match his bewilderment.

I smiled, "well, in your defense, you were in your mother's stomach at the time."

He reciprocated my smile with his own.

"And how old is Thomas?" I hoped asking his age made this seem more routine.

"Twenty-four." His expression changed again as he thought about his little brother. A warmth came over him and resulted in his cheeks rising slightly from an easy to miss quick smile.

"Is Christine your sister?" My case file on the Turner's never mentioned Christine. Only the two boys were noted as descendants of Jeremiah and Margaret.

This brought out a full laugh from Ezekiel. I joined in not knowing what else to do. "She's only a few years younger than my mom." He had trouble getting it all out as he laughed through his response.

I nodded acknowledging how ridiculous it must have sounded to him. The question remained though, "who is she?"

The same warmth he expressed talking about his brother returned as he spoke about Christine. "I've known her all my life. She was like a second mom to me. Well, more of a friend than another mom." His head lowered and his eyes began to get watery again.

I sat back a little and placed the note pad back in my pocket. We were getting to something. He was on the verge of sharing critical information. I've seen it many times. The next question would likely result in him shutting down or feeling comfortable enough to share something that is causing him significant pain.

I lowered my voice to mirror the angst Ezekiel was feeling. "Where is Christine now?"

His shoulders lifted and fell with no words accompanying his movements. He didn't know. His eyes stayed locked on to mine reinforcing the authenticity of his statement.

All kinds of thoughts flooded my head as I worked through the scenarios. Christine was close to Margaret's age. Was there something more between Jeremiah and Christine? Did Margaret become jealous. Love. Jealousy. They were often the ingredients to drive a violent emotional response. I didn't want to be accusatory given Ezekiel seemed to care dearly for this woman. In the same caring tone as before, I asked a follow up question. "Where is your mom?"

Ezekiel expressed the same look combined with the shoulder shrug. He looked like a teenager not comfortable talking to an adult. I couldn't believe what he was sharing. I was sent here based on the report of a missing person, Jeremiah Turner. Is it possible there are three people missing? Why weren't they reported?

I pulled my note pad wanting to capture the answer to the next question. I flipped to a new page. "When was the last time you saw Christine?"

Ezekiel looked at my notepad as he spoke, "Sunday. Sunday before church."

I wrote Sunday AM next to Christine's name. "When was the last time you saw your mom?"

He continued staring at the small piece of paper in my hand. "Sunday evening."

Next to Margaret's name I etched in Sunday PM. "And your dad, when did you last see him?"

His answer was much longer this time. "We all had lunch together. The four of us that is. It wasn't any different than any other Sunday other than Christine was not with us. We went for a ride around the property while mom cleaned up the dishes. It was just another Sunday."

He's missing something. Details. It happens, emotions cloud our memories. "Did your dad or mom talk at lunch about Christine? Did they wonder where she might be since she normally eats with the family?"

Ezekiel did not respond immediately. You could see he was replaying the events in his head. It had been more than 48 hours and it was such a mundane event at the time. "Dad rarely spoke at lunch. He did this past Sunday. He asked us if we had seen Christine. I remember now. Thomas and I responded, no sir, but mom never responded. It upset dad."

Did Margaret know something? Was she covering for Christine? "Ezekiel, I am going to ask you something.

Something personal about your family. I am sure you have been raised properly to avoid such talk. But it is important. It may help us locate your mom and dad. "Did your dad anger easily? Would he get physical with any of you?"

Ezekiel's eyelids were fluttering while his fingers began quietly tapping on the bed frame. He didn't have to respond to the question. I already knew the answer. "He never touched Thomas or me." His answer a vindication and incrimination all at the same time.

I nodded my head and placed my hand on his shoulder again. He erupted as the tears began flowing from his eyes. I moved from the chair and knelt on one knee by his side. I placed my arm around him. He fell into me like a child that needed a warm place to land. This young man was dealing with a tremendous amount of grief. I saw it occur far too often when I served in the military. The immortality all of us feel when we are young, ripped away suddenly when something happens unexpectedly to a friend or family member. We always believe we will have more time to make things right.

The comforting embrace resulted in Ezekiel collecting himself enough to continue. He regained his focus. "What else can I do to help, Sheriff?"

I returned to the chair knowing Ezekiel wanted to continue. I thought for a moment before responding. "The ride. Did anything out of the ordinary happen?"

It was clear Ezekiel was a contemplative young man. He chose his words carefully and, at least in this interview, answered thoughtfully. I wondered if this was a result of being raised in a house with someone that angered easily. Measured responses had become a habit. A survival technique. "The ride was longer than most Sundays. We went through areas of the property we do not usually ride. Moses was tiring from all the exercise. Moses is my…"

"I've met Moses. He's a good horse. He allowed an old man like me to ride him without throwing me off." I smiled again to bring back a little levity to the conversation. It was critical to keep his emotions in check.

Ezekiel nodded and smiled, "Yes sir. He is a good horse. I was having trouble keeping up with dad. The last place we stopped at was the well. Dad got there before me and trotted around the perimeter of the clearing. He could see Moses was laboring. Well, more than usual for an old horse. He told me to walk him back to the barn. We usually rode back together. His horse was the only thing that returned later that evening."

I made a note of the last location Jeremiah was seen by his son. The well. "You said you saw your mom that evening. Anything out of the ordinary?

He ran his fingers through his hair and replied. "No. She was preparing dinner. We always had stew on Sunday for dinner. She chopped the ingredients, placed them in the large pot and put it on the fire. The smell would fill the cabin for two hours as it roasted. Mom went to the well as usual to retrieve water for dinner and our nightly chores." The well. I placed an asterisk next to the location. The repetition of the location made it a high priority for my investigation.

I could sense I had mined most of the critical information from the young man. Unless I asked more specific questions, we would just be regurgitating the same information. I didn't know what else to ask given I had limited knowledge of the case.

"Anything else you would recommend I look into while I am here?" An open-ended question was always a good catchall to conclude an interview.

This time Ezekiel did not hesitate. "I would check two places Sheriff. Dad's workshop and my grandparent's cabin. Christine would occasionally sleep there when she wasn't allowed in our cabin." The words implied the disciplinary nature of the banishment.

The two did seem like worthwhile locations for obvious reasons, but I wondered if he pointed them out for something more directly related to the case. I waited to see if he would expand on his suggestion to investigate both locations. No further response came. He seemed exhausted. I am sure he has not slept in the two days since his life was turned upside down. I decided I had put him through enough for one interview. I could always come back once I had more specific items to follow up on. Ezekiel was going to be an ally for me to rely on when I needed him.

"Do you mind if I have a moment to look around the cabin alone?" It is highly unusual to have a citizen observe a search.

"Of course. I need to get on with my morning chores anyway." Ezekiel was very accommodating. He stood and reached his hand to me.

We exchanged handshakes and I watched him leave his home. I was going to give a cursory search of the premises but more importantly I wanted to capture my thoughts uninterrupted.

I flipped to a new page and jotted down the following.

Christine missing first. Why? Where did she go? Margaret seemed to know something.

Jeremiah went missing next. Last seen at the well.

Margaret went missing last. She went to the well to retrieve water.

Why did they all go missing on the same day? How could three people disappear without a trace?

Chapter 14: Reunited

I felt a soft touch on my skin. Fingers caressing me as they moved up and down my arm. It wasn't the rough and rigid feel of my son's hands. Someone else was in the underground home with me.

I slowly opened my eyes to see a young woman sitting next to me. A smile spread across her face.

"You're awake! Billy will be so happy when he gets back. He is out gathering food for dinner". She clapped her hands together in front of her in anticipation.

The girl took my hand in her arms and brought it up to her face. She pressed it against the side of her cheek.

I swallowed in preparation to talk to her. "Laura? Are you Billy's Laura?" For the most part, the child like features I remembered were hidden in the young woman's face.

Laura's smile widened enough to expose her teeth. "Yes, Billy's friend. And you are the lady in the woods. Billy's mom."

I couldn't help but smile even though the pain of my injuries were starting to register again. "Lady in the woods? You make it sound like a fairy tale."

Laura placed my hands together on my stomach before responding. "I thought of you as the Fairy Godmother of the woods. I wasn't sure you were even real until I met Billy again a few years ago. I thought I had made both of you up to cope with all the abuse I had endured."

Her words made me think about that time in my life. The hiding. Escaping from the physical abuse I experienced in the Commune. The short excursions to the woods to nurture my boy as best I could given the circumstances. She experienced the same abuse as a child. She hid in the woods for the same reasons, to have a short respite from the cruelty inflicted by evil people. "You were always such a strong and self-reliant child."

She placed her hands around mine and moved closer to my face. "Billy gave me my strength. He saved my life twice. Without you, there would be no Billy, and I would not be here." She leaned closer and softly kissed my forehead before returning to a kneeling position at my side.

It was comforting to hear Billy protected Laura. I must have done something right to have instilled this in him. I regret not doing more for both Laura and Billy. I should have done more to remove them from the people that caused them so much pain. "I'm sorry Laura." She tried to stop me, but I had to get it out. It has weighed on me like many of the other decisions I made along the way. "No. I need to say this to you. The two of you deserved more help from an adult. I let you down the same as all the other adults in your life. I should have kept trying to get the two you to a safe place."

Laura's expression suggested she appreciated what I said while not agreeing with it completely. "Please don't take this the wrong way." She placed her hand on my forehead and intertwined her fingers in my hair. As she lightly tasseled my locks back and forth, she continued speaking in a more serious tone. "I love Billy. We both know he could never make it outside of this world. He would never be accepted. He would never be able to function in that world. You did the right thing by keeping him here. And everything you did, including not helping me, was all to protect your son. I would have done the same thing in your shoes." Laura stopped her words before finishing her thought. "I made the same choice for Billy."

I turned away from Laura as her hand slid off to the side. Her words were both comforting and upsetting. I attempted to hide the tears that began to flow from my eyes. Did she know about his rage? What he has done to the others that angered him? It was very considerate of her to try and justify my actions. She was much further along than I was in forgiving all that has occurred. Maybe I will get there. Maybe I will agree with her one day. Everything I have done was driven by what was best for Billy. I continued to look away as I softly said through the lingering tears, "Thank you."

It must have been clear to Laura now that I was crying. I felt her nestle in beside me on the blanket. She wrapped her right arm around me and placed her head on my shoulder. I pulled her close to me with my left arm. Her weight accentuated the pain I felt in some of my sore areas, but it didn't stop me from wanting the moment to last. I closed my eyes and was thankful Billy had someone like Laura in his life. I'm not sure what would have happened to my son without her.

As if that wasn't enough, she tried to console me even more. "There, there." She stopped abruptly. "I don't think I know your real name. Unless you want me to keep referring to you as the lady in the woods or Fairy Godmother."

I turned my head back to hers. My left arm crossing over my body to her long brown hair. I brought my mouth to her forehead. "I guess Lady of the Woods is too formal." The tears were now intermittent, and the words caused us both to shake a little from laughter. "Christine. My name is Christine Ferguson." It felt good saying it aloud. With Margaret gone, Laura is now just one of a few people that know my name.

Laura continued, "Billy Ferguson. I never knew his last name. All this time." I didn't think it was appropriate to correct her in the moment. Technically, his name should be Billy Wallace, after his father. I guess I can decide his name since there is no birth certificate. Johnny meant a lot to me, but I had raised Billy all these years. It wasn't his choice to abandon his son, but it didn't change the reality of the situation. Billy was a Ferguson.

Laura returned her attention to me. "There, there Christine. Rest easy. All three of us have made it!" I couldn't help but think Laura was wise beyond her years. It was almost as if we had reversed roles. She was consoling me. She and Billy were both resilient. A product of all they have endured over the years.

I kissed Laura's head the same as she had done to mine. "You are an amazing person. You have overcome so much."

Laura did not leave much space between our words. "You..." She paused, "you have been strong for so much long."

I didn't want the moment to end. It was not often I had a genuine moment of intimacy with another person. I held Laura tight trying to deflect the other thoughts racing through my head. How long had she been living in this underground world with Billy? Does she have family or people outside of the woods looking for her. I regret not being able to leave the Commune to spend one more day with dad before he passed. I hope she isn't sacrificing the same for Billy. She must know there is no future for her here. I could not let her go down the same path I took so many years ago. And I could not allow her to be harmed should Billy become enraged. I know this now about my son.

Both of our heads looked up as Billy had quietly made his way into the room. "Mawmee!" My son joined the two of us in a prolonged embrace. The physical discomfort intensified but it was more than offset by the love I felt in my heart. I had my son in my right arm and his good friend on the other side of me. The three of us together for the first time in more than twenty years. I was crying and smiling at the same time, alternating kisses on each of their foreheads. The first time since we made the pact in the woods for Billy and Laura to protect one another. "Above ground rules."

Billy responded like a child answering his teacher's prompt in school. "Pwotect Lauwa."

"Protect Billy." Laura replied immediately after Billy.

Like a ball being thrown back and forth between two people, Billy continued. "Know the cave."

"Rule three, only exit and enter the cave through the same place." Laura's tone implied she was surprised to have remembered the exact words.

Billy paused before attempting to share rule four. "No one, see you, in or out of cave."

I jumped in before Laura could share the final rule. I said the words deliberately to emphasize their importance. "Never go inside the wall in the woods."

Chapter 15: Kindred Spirits

My physical condition was improving with each day that passed. I was now able to move around in the underground cave and help Laura with the daily chores. Her activities limited by an impairment affecting the full use of her legs. She had to rest often given the extra effort to complete each task. It felt good to help her. She has done so much for my son over the years.

Billy spent much of his time out in the woods. It was obvious he was worried. He would mutter in broken sentences about men riding horses in the area. I knew it was Simon and his gang searching for Jeremiah. Once again, I had put my child, and now Laura, in danger by coming to the cave. Billy was observing their movements to make sure they were not closing in on our location. I cautioned him to be careful on each of his forays into the woods. I endured so much pain at the hands of Simon and his brothers. If Billy knew this, he would kill every last one of them.

Billy's excursions left large chunks of time for the two of us to get to know each other. "Laura, I noticed you look at a book each night before we go to sleep." I hoped the unfinished sentence would trigger a dialogue.

She seemed embarrassed that I had noticed her reading. Perhaps she thought I was already asleep when she flipped through the pages. Laura nodded her head in lieu of a verbal response.

"Don't be ashamed sweetie. It's okay if you do not want to share what you read each night. I didn't mean to impose." I placed my hand on her shoulder to further demonstrate my understanding.

Laura did not respond leaving me to assume the book was very personal to her. I turned to rest on the blanket when I noticed her retrieving a bag from a crevice in the side of the underground cavern. I hadn't even noticed it until the light from the candle penetrated the opening.

She brought the entire bag over to me and placed the candle by our side. She reached in and pulled out several small black books. I immediately recognized them as the diaries I had given to Billy years ago. They were a gift from Margaret. A gift to give to my son on his 5th birthday.

"I can't believe it. I gave these to Billy." I placed my fingers on the cover of the first book and slowly slid them over the weathered cover. Every crack and groove explored by my fingertips. The lines not unsimilar to those that traverse the skin on the back of my hand.

Laura smiled. "Billy gave one to me. This one."

My son had shared one of the few possessions he had with his childhood friend. I wasn't sure how Laura would respond, but I asked anyway. "Show me?"

Laura did not hesitate. She opened to the first page. It was a drawing from when she was very young. I watched her grow up as she flipped through the pages. Laura would point out Billy in many of the drawings. He was always hidden and yet always present. I wouldn't have noticed him had she not identified him hidden in the pictures. A photograph dropped from the pages of the diary. She tried to hide it from me as she picked it up from atop the blanket. She knew I had seen the image before she could return it between the pages. It was Laura when she much younger standing beside a disheveled looking woman. The woman's face had been scratched out and a red x mark over her body. "This woman here," she pointed to the disfigured side of the photo, "this woman was my birth mom."

"It wasn't your fault that she hit you Laura." Laura nodded her head while still staring at the photo. "Why did you keep it all this time?"

"It's the only image of me before I went to grade school." I took the picture from her hand and place it between the two of the pages we had already viewed.

"You should keep it. It's part of your story."

Laura flipped ahead with each page containing more and more words. She was growing up as each page turned. It was evident she had made new friends. Billy was still watching from afar in her drawings. She documented the abuse she received at the hands of her birth mom. I couldn't help but feel the same rage that drove Billy to confront her.

Laura filled in many details well beyond what was depicted on each page. She did this especially when the story revolved around Billy. It was good to hear he had some normalcy in his childhood. They played house in the small structure in the woods. They played "hidenseek" often. Her revelations overwhelmed me. I placed my hand over my mouth to suppress any sound that might escape. Tears flowed from eyes and gathered around the top of my index finger. I must have hidden my reaction well as Laura continued telling stories with each page. I felt joy as a parent. The joy you feel when you know your child is happy.

Laura made it to the last few pages of the diary. It was evident it was written when she was much older. Laura handed the bound book to me to read the last page.

It started with a letter and was followed by a brief list of things she was thankful for in her life. The letter conveyed her desire to keep the woods from being sold. It was clear it was to protect Billy. Protect the area in order to hide his existence. The magnitude of the sacrifice she made for my son was overwhelming.

I reached over and pulled Laura close to me as I read through the list. The first name listed was her mom. It wasn't about the woman that gave birth to her and abused her for years. It was about the woman that adopted her and gave her a loving home. "Tell me about her."

Laura launched into story after story about Jean Perry. The mom that raised her after adopting her when she was just eleven years old. She missed her mom. I sensed it was the same as my yearning to see my dad again. The desire has never faded to feel the unconditional love when wrapped up in one of his bear hugs.

The next name on the list was a Sheriff named Jack Conway. I didn't know him. We rarely had unknown visitors at the Commune. He also made sacrifices for Laura. I could see why he meant so much to her. He was the conduit for getting Laura to Jean. She described Sheriff Conway as a civil servant with a moral compass that far exceeded the requirements of the job.

The next name brought out a little laughter as I read it. "You had a friend named Christie!" It was very close to my name. Laura had met Christie in college. The two roommates became best friends. Hearing her talk about this time in her life reminded me of Johnny, Billy's dad. He was only a freshmen in college when we met. I remember how we both had so much to look forward to at this age. It was difficult not to imagine what Johnny was doing with his life. He was a driven and passionate young man. I am sure he has accomplished amazing things.

The next name was Luke. I remember him from the drawings. He was a childhood friend that came into Laura's life after she had met Billy. I wondered how Luke's and Laura's friendship affected Billy. I could hear the emotion in her voice as she described their relationship and his tragic death on the train trestle. It made sense to me now. Those years were tough on Billy. I had no idea what he was experiencing. He would never share why but I knew something had made him angry for several years. I now understand why. Luke's death ultimately set in motion the events that removed Laura from the toxic home where she was raised. The train incident saved her life even though it unfortunately ended another. It also left my son alone and without his only friend.

"Billy." I read the last name on the list. I pulled Laura even closer knowing Billy meant so much to her. "My guardian angel." It is what she had scribed next to his name. The words inspired me. I had seen people use religion to defend their own beliefs and justify their own actions. My son had overcome a tremendous amount of challenges. Most of the challenges he overcame on his own. He still had within him the heart to care for someone else. To put their needs above his own. I closed the diary. "Thank you for sharing your story with me Laura. I could never repay you for the new memories you have given me. Memories of my son's childhood that I never knew before today."

Laura pulled away a little from me and had a somewhat devious smirk on her face.

I hesitated before reacting, "what?" I had no idea where this was going.

She took a deep breath, "I want to record your story." She shuffled through the bag and found one journal that had yet to contain any writing. She held it close to her chest and begged, "please!"

I could only think of one word, "why?"

"Your story is Billy's story. He should know it when he's ready. I would like to give it to him as a gift. The whole story." Laura was now on her knees prodding me to go along with the request.

Both positive and negative reactions filled my head as I sorted through the unexpected request. I thought of a compromise. "I will tell you my story. You can record it in the diary." Laura excitedly nodded her head not even knowing what else I might say. "You must let me decide, after we have finished, if Billy should ever see it."

Laura agreed to the terms as verified by her warm embrace. Both of her arms wrapped around my body for a quick hug.

She wasted no time getting started. Opening to page one she asked a simple question. "Where did Billy come from?"

I sat back and began sharing my journey. Laura furiously penned each word. Pages filled and were turned as the words flowed. It was cathartic. The life of Christine Ferguson and the birth of her son. Hours passed as the number of remaining blank pages plunged to just a few.

Laura abruptly stopped writing and closed the diary. "We are kindred spirits." I could see the many parallels having shared my story aloud. Two people from worlds apart experiencing similar journeys. The two of us driven to protect the same person at all costs. A person that truly had no other confidant to rely on.

Laura replaced the diaries in the bag and returned them to the hiding place. As she positioned them far back in the crevice she recommitted to her promise. "I will only share these with Billy with your permission and when the time is right."

She made her way back over to me as we rested on the blanket. Laura opened and closed her right hand several times to stretch the ligaments and tendons fatigued from the excessive amount of writing.

I took her hand in mine and began to massage the joints to soothe the pain. Kneading each finger and her palm as we stared at one another. Our bond had been Billy. Now it was so much more.

Our focus was brought to the entrance of the room as we began to hear noises from someone approaching. We blew out the candle and shuffled back to the far recesses of the underground space. Billy was always quiet with his movements. He would often be standing beside us before we knew he was in the room. This realization only heightened our growing concern.

The disturbance outside had now moved inside the hidden room. Laura's fingers dug into my arm as she pulled even closer to me. I did my best to remain calm for her benefit.

The sound of a match dragging across a rough surface echoed in the space. A flash of light followed but moved much to quickly for us to make out the trespasser. The flame grew as it was transferred to a torch. It illuminated the face of the intruder.

We both called out at the same time. "Billy!" We rushed to his side as he seemed out of sorts. He collapsed in our arms while transferring the torch to Laura.

We lowered him to the blanket and moved the torch by his side. He was sweating profusely as if he had been running a great distance. His ragged pants displayed a growing red splotch on his left leg. He had been injured somehow. I grabbed a piece of cloth and applied pressure to his thigh. He reached up for both of us as we hovered over him.

"Billy, how did this happen?" I kept the pressure on his leg as I inquired about his injury. I wanted to keep him conscious and alert. I also needed to know how all this happened and if we were in any immediate danger.

He muttered only a couple of barely discernable words. "The howse men." Billy's eyes were fluttering as he strained to keep them open. "Gun shots. Ran. Fell. Howt leg."

I took his hand in mine and looked him in the eyes. "Did they see you enter the cave?" Laura went to the entrance of the room to see if he had been followed.

Billy shook his head slowly. I exhaled. Billy uttered another terrifying statement, "gettin' close."

Laura returned from the entrance. "No sign of anyone. Is he going to be alright?" Tears were now falling from her eyes.

As much as I wanted to reassure her, I didn't know. Billy closed his eyes and was non-responsive to our attempts to wake him. His chest was rising and falling but at a much slower rate than usual.

"Get scissors, needle and string from the bag." Laura scurried away to collect the items. I removed the cloth from Billy's leg and began to investigate the source and severity of the wound. I lit a candle with the torch light and brought it to within inches of his leg. Seeing the injury up close added to the anxiety I was feeling. I could tell it caused an even greater reaction from Laura. I had to keep her busy in case I needed her. "Get the water we boiled last night on the fire."

Laura returned with the bucket of water. I began to cut away the blood-stained section of Billy's pants. I snipped the last piece exposing the full extent of the injury. The wound indicated it was pierced by something. Billy must have had his leg impaled when he fell. The jagged cut was most likely from a stick or branch. I leaned in closer to see remnants of the bark dispersed along the wound. The opening was several inches long but fortunately not very deep. Regardless, it bled significantly for the size of the wound.

I shook my hands and fingers to express the pent-up nerves so I could function with more precision. I wrapped the cloth I had cut away from the pants around Billy's leg just above the wound. I pulled it tight reducing the flow of blood exiting his body. "Give me the string." Simon's wife had me assist several times when she stitched up minor injuries. I never did the procedure by myself. I took another deep breath and said softly, "you can do this, you must do this for your son."

Laura looked away as I began attempting to close the wound. Billy did not move. He was still unconscious from losing so much blood. Each pass of the string pulled the skin together. I tied off the string and cut off the excess. I gently loosened the cloth above the wound to see if the stitches were enough to hold it closed. Only a minimal amount of blood was seeping through the now fused skin.

"We need to clean the wound and bandage it to keep if from getting infected." The request brought Laura's eyes back to Billy's injured leg.

The two of us began gently washing the area with cloths using the purified water. We did the best we could and then wrapped it gently with a fresh dressing. "We need to make a fire. We need to keep Billy warm."

Laura started shuffling around before stopping in her tracks. "If someone enters the cave they might see or smell the fire." She was noticeably scared.

"I know. It's a risk. But we need to take care of Billy. He is the priority and he would do the same for either of us." Laura nodded and went back to prepping for the fire.

The temperature in the room increased with the heat from the flames. We had enough wood to last through the night. Billy would always replenish it each day on his morning expeditions through the woods. "We should lie down next to him. It will keep him warm and let him know we are both here with him."

We moved in beside him and formed and extra layer of insulation surrounding his body. I stretched my arm completely across Billy and placed it on the back of Laura's head. I ran my fingers through her hair to calm her fears. "He will be okay."

A few minutes quietly passed. The time gave my mind a chance to catch up with all that had occurred.

Simon and his gang are closing in on our location. Billy may have left tracks to the cave given his injuries. I have no idea if they clearly saw what they were shooting at in the woods. I have no idea if they will pursue the lead further. I cannot take that chance. I cannot risk all of us being found. If Billy awakens before nightfall, I will need to protect him. I might only have one more night to do something.

I closed my eyes. What can I do? I have never been able to completely protect him. I have failed miserably getting him out of this situation. I have the shotgun but no practice using it. It will make a lot of noise. The attention will give me almost no chance of escaping the walls of the Commune. I'll be questioned if captured. Probably killed during the interrogation. Either way, I will be jeopardizing Billy and Laura's chances of surviving.

I must kill Simon. He is their leader. The whole Commune will wither away and die with him out of the picture. But how? I didn't have it in me when I had the chance to end Jeremiah's pathetic reign. I had the scissors pressed against his body. All it took was one push and I could have enacted the revenge I had envisioned for years. Margaret had to step in and pull the trigger for me.

I moved my hand from Laura's hair and placed it on Billy's chest. He was still breathing. Still fighting. Laura was now quietly resting at his side.

A thought raced through my head. It played out in my mind like a scene from a movie. I could see it. A smile came to my face. I knew how I could get Simon. I knew how I could go undetected. I wouldn't even be in the same place when he takes his final breath. And I knew, that if I were successful, my son would be safe once and for all.

Chapter 16: Closing In

I exited the room to find Elijah waiting for me on the stairs of the cabin. He sarcastically greeted me, "Well Sheriff, I've been waiting for 45 minutes. Did you find my brother in his cabin?"

The ridiculous question did not deserve a response. "I need to interview everyone. Where is Simon and the others?"

"Well, you see Sheriff, they're on patrols. Searching every inch of the woods that surround the Commune. They didn't think it likely to find him hiding under his bed." Elijah made it to his feet as he finished his second attempt at mocking my activities.

I stared longer than usual at Elijah before continuing the conversation. "Who all is helping Simon? Searching?" I took my pad out to record the names.

"Well, I should be one of them instead of babysitting…" His tone was getting more aggressive, so I cut him off mid-sentence.

"I'm here at Simon's request. He gave me permission to conduct this investigation." I was tired of playing this game.

Elijah looked away knowing I had the high ground. Elijah would have to answer to Simon if I reported his antics. "Leroy Davis, Lester McElroy and Frankie Whitfield. They have all been members of the church for many years." He answered reluctantly finally giving me the information I needed.

"Did all three-attend church this past Sunday?" It was important to know if they were on the premises when the others went missing.

Elijah shook his head, "Yes. They attend church every Sunday. It is not an option for those of us that believe."

"Whitfield? The owner of the Town Diner?" I knew the answer but asked anyway.

Elijah turned back to me and gave a look demonstrating he was aware of my condescending question. "YES, SIR!" He said it loudly as his irritation was growing.

I made a note and left space for my eventual interview with Mr. Whitfield. "Tell me about the other two." I flipped the page to give more space to fill in future details.
"Leroy is my brother-in-law. Married Simon's daughter a few years ago after a long courtship. The two of them live in one of the newer cabins on the property. Lester lives up the road with his wife. His family has been involved with the church going back to the early years when my dad was pastor." I knew

of the property he was referring to on Pope Lick Road.

"Is that all?" Elijah didn't give me a lot of details, only the essentials. I figured I would have to get more directly from the individuals.

Elijah's lack of a response told me he was not going to divulge any more than he already had in the contentious exchange. "Where to next Sheriff?"

I need to radio Sheriff Wagner. The scope of the investigation has changed. Keeping this from him would be a violation of our agreement. "I have to get something from my truck and then I would like to see Jeremiah's workshop." I wasn't going to let Elijah know anything more than what was necessary.

Elijah moved to his horse without answering. I guess that was his way of agreeing to my request. I moved quickly to get a few extra seconds since mounting Moses was a chore. Elijah was already riding off as I circled around the old horse. Before Elijah disappeared, I made it on top of the saddle. I gave Moses a little nudge to race after the other horse.

I didn't catch up until we arrived back at the church. I had forgotten how taxing riding a horse was on the body. I slid off the side with a little more polish than before. I was starting to get the hang of this mode of transportation again. Elijah went into the church giving me a window to contact the Sheriff.

The truck door creaked loudly potentially blowing my cover. Fortunately, the grassy field was empty. There wasn't a soul in sight. I slid behind the wheel and gave the ignition a quarter turn. Just enough juice to allow me to make a quick call. I kept the two-way radio below my chest to hide it from anyone outside of my truck. I pushed the call button. "Sheriff Wagner, do you read me?"

I released the button while looking around the area. Scanning from left to right to see if anyone had made there way out into the field. It remained serene along with any response from the other end of the call. I pushed the button again and repeated the question.

Another minute passed with no response. I began to replace the corded mic back on the unit when the call response came. "I hear you Deputy. What's the update? Over."

"I need another 24 hours. I have interviewed Ezekiel Turner the son of Jeremiah and Margaret Turner. His statement has changed everything. Over." I knew the update would likely trigger the Sheriff to bring the entire department to the Commune. He might even reach out to our friends in Jefferson County for more resources.

The static between calls provided exclamation points to each of our exchanges. "Jack, I can only hold off for so long. What have you learned? Over."

I hesitated with my response. "There is more than just one person missing. Jeremiah's wife and a friend of the family are also MIA. Over." I took a deep breath as I dropped my hand and the two-way radio to my lap.

"Three missing people! Jack, you know what this means. The chances of foul play are almost a certainty. Over." His voice thundered over the radio.

"I know. I know, sir. If you bring the cavalry now, we will cut off all communication with the remaining material witnesses. Enemies always retract when they are threatened. I have Simon's blessing to conduct a full investigation. I will stay the night and work through the day tomorrow. If I am no further along by this time tomorrow, you can bring everyone. Over." I looked up to the roof of the truck and closed my eyes hoping Sheriff Wagner would give me the additional time I needed.

"24 hours Jack. You have until Wednesday at 6pm. I can't have you out there on your own. You need back-up. A lot could go wrong if you get too close to figuring this out on your own. Someone may try to take matters into their own hands. Not only putting you in danger but risking the loss of everything you have uncovered. Over." The static came through the air waves once again.

He seemed genuinely concerned about my well-being. Any blood shed would be on his hands. Whatever his motivation, his response was appropriate. He was giving me what I wanted even though everything has escalated beyond what we had anticipated. I exhaled and responded, "thank you." I paused before concluding, "Over."

I was pulled back into the conversation with another question. "What's the name of the friend. The friend of the family? I will begin to establish her file. Over."

We should learn more about this woman. It could help determine why she went missing with the Turner's. It was the behind the scenes admin work involved in every case. It wasn't glamorous, but just as important as the field work. "Her name is Christine Ferguson. Based on Ezekiel's statement she should be around fifty years old. I know you know this, but you must keep your research confidential Sheriff. You know what happens to me if word gets back to Simon. If he knows we are pursuing the other individuals that are missing, it could jeopardize everything. We have the upper hand if he thinks we are only looking for Jeremiah. Over."

"Roger that Jack. I'll do the research myself. I can't trust that ass hat Curtis to get me coffee, let alone something this important. Be careful and report in tomorrow. Over and out." The last burst of white noise blasted through the com device. I returned it to the holster silencing the racket.

My rear-view mirror caught Elijah coming out of the church. I opened the door and started walking in his direction. I had to shout as we were further away from one another for a normal conversation. "The workshop." I have wasted enough time. I am on the clock. And the clock is ticking.

Elijah stopped moving in my direction. "It's just down that path. It's the only structure on that side of the property. You will see it on the right side just past the large willow tree. No reason to ride."

He was encouraging me to go alone. I was suspicious of his motives for relinquishing me to investigate the area on my own. I pointed towards the path and began walking in the direction of the purported workshop. I listened closely for any movement behind me. Nothing.

As I made my way to the tree-line, I glance back over my shoulder. I waited to get to this distance hoping it would be less obvious. Elijah was no longer standing in the field. I visually inspected the area to the left and right of the church. He was nowhere to be found. I unclasped the strap holstering my gun and raised it to my side. I continued down the path on full alert.

Nature filled the area with its rhythmic sounds, rising and falling in intensity. Guardedly progressing through the area while watching for any signs that I was being followed. Still nothing. Instinctively, I brought my gun out in front of me. I was now cutoff from the church and where my truck was located. If I were being setup, now would be the time to attack. I would have little chance of escaping. I proceeded with caution. Each step pausing briefly to determine if any other movements were occurring around me. My eyes moving from side to side as I searched the thick brush surrounding the narrow road.

It seemed like hours when I reached a small clearing off to my right. I turned and looked back over my shoulder. My movements purposeful and deliberate. All indications were that I was alone in the woods. I approached the small structure assuming it was the workshop Ezekiel recommended searching.

I tapped the door with my gun three times. I stepped back and moved into a squatting position. Smaller target should someone come rushing out. No response.

I raised up and made my way to the door. I kept the gun in my right hand, pointed in front of me, as I reached out with my left hand. I grasped the handle and slowly pulled the door to me. I quickly pointed the gun inside the space alternating where I aimed. My eyes darting to each corner of the room.

The workshop was clear.

I relaxed my posture and repositioned the gun by my side. I stood upright to stretch my back. I began the process of investigating the space.

The bench in front of me was covered with dust and powdery substances. Rows of narrow shelving were behind the bench extending all the way to the ceiling. Bottles and containers lined the wooden ledges. I began picking out random items and reviewing the contents. A man-made label was affixed to most of them with a barely legible inscription on each one. I didn't recognize most of the words, but it was clear they were medications. Some in pill form and some grounded into a powder. I began recording their names in my note pad.

Workshop. This is not what I was expecting. I wasn't aware of any medical training in Jeremiah's past. It made sense to have supplies given how isolated the Commune was from the closest medical facility, but this was more like an entire pharmacy than a first aid station. I completed an inventory of every container. I recorded over 60 drugs. Some of the names were hyphenated and were clearly concoctions of multiple medications. I recognized a few from my military exploits. Drugs that were prescribed to men to enhance their battle readiness. Benzedrine. The enlisted men referred to it as the "wake up" pill. It was later to be classified as an amphetamine and pulled from use due to its addictive nature. As much as I loved serving my country, it was difficult to reconcile some of the methods we used to prepare our men for battle and the toll it took on them afterward.

Why would Jeremiah have drugs that were no longer being prescribed? Why would he mix Benzedrine with other drugs? Benze-Thalidomide? Where would he get access to these banned pharmaceuticals? My worst fears of this place were being confirmed. First, Ezekiel's description of the abuse Margaret and Christine endured, and now the discovery of an illegal drug lab. The polished veneer stripped away to uncover rotten wood just below the surface. I sat down on the wooden planks that made up the floor of the small room. I couldn't believe what I was unearthing. I couldn't believe that individuals were subjected to abuse and maybe worse while I had jurisdiction over their safety. I brought my hand to my face and covered my mouth. It saddened me. All my work, all these years – to protect and to serve. To fight for those that could not fight for themselves. And yet, I had let them down. It took a moment to collect myself before I slowly moved to a standing position. I was reminded of every ache and pain a lifetime of service had inflicted on my body. Adjusting my uniform, I stared at the door to the cabin.

When I walk though that door, I will step out and finish my final mission. I owe it to those I let down. I will never be at peace with my calling if I don't give this my maximum effort. I cannot go back, but I can act now. My subconscious thoughts galvanized my resolve.

I stepped forward feeling no pain. My mindset had changed. I saw men in my unit fight and try to walk after having their legs severely injured from an attack. They never conceded because they were laser focused on their mission. They put all other thoughts out of their mind. This is what it takes to survive. This is what it takes to overcome the enemy.

I swung the door open to see Elijah standing on the road.

I walked past him not even pausing to acknowledge his presence. "Your parent's cabin." Elijah had to quicken his pace to catch up. "Your brother. The workshop. Why did he have it?" Direct and in control. It was time for me to wield the power I carried as a deputy of the Shelby County Sheriff's office.

Elijah was not ready for this line of questioning. He was also struggling to catch his breath from how fast we were moving through the woods. "You know. Hobby."

"Fishing and hunting is a hobby. Riding horses or hiking are hobbies. Playing with illicit drugs is not." Call a spade a spade and force Elijah into a corner. Would he defend his brother?

"He." He stopped speaking and took a few more steps before continuing. "Jeremiah saw himself as an apothecary. He treated many of us on the Commune when we were ill or injured. I think if he could have left the Commune, he would have pursued work in the medical field."

Both thoughts were equally terrifying. Jeremiah as a doctor in the real world and an untrained Jeremiah playing one inside these walls. "Where did he get all of his supplies?"

"I'm afraid you would have to ask him that question." Elijah's breathing added to his need to keep his statements brief.

He was withholding information. He was not going to incriminate his brother, or the life people lived at the Commune. Elijah is still not respecting the authority represented by the badge on my chest. I would have to be more aggressive. Put him in his place to physically show him I have the power to take them all down. As I prepped my movements to force him to the ground, I stopped in my tracks upon hearing a noise coming from the woods.

It was growing louder and louder. Emerging from the brush, the patrol had finished their last ride of the day. The four men guided their horses up to our side. The signs of their exhaustion were evident. Sweat stains dampened much of the material that covered their upper body.

Simon, as usual, initiated the dialogue. "Sheriff, discover anything that might help us find my brother?"

Be delicate. Continue to earn his trust. Thoughts converged on how to best answer his question. "Ruling things out at this point. Process of elimination."

Simon expressed some air through his mouth with what sounded like a soft chuckle. "Things?" His tone conveyed he knew I was talking about people.

I was picking up on an odor that was all too familiar. Gun powder. At least one of their firearms had been used and used recently. "What about your patrol. Did you find anything?"

As Simon was preparing to respond, I attempted to locate the weapon that had been discharged. "Out of the mouth of babes and sucklings, hast thou ordained strength because of thine enemies, that thou mightiest still the enemy and the avenger."

The last thing I wanted to hear was more sermonizing from Simon. I narrowed down the weapon to one of two riders that were on my left. "Your firearm. It has been discharged recently. Did you see something?" It was bold especially since I was outnumbered five to one.

The question seemed to perplex the youngest of the riders. As if he were astonished, I could tell such a thing from just walking next to him. He looked over at Simon before responding.

Simon nodded. He didn't have much choice. If he shook his head, it would certainly raise red flags and lead to more questioning.

The man who looked to be in his early fifties shared the circumstances that led to him firing his weapon. "I saw something. Something moving through the woods. Barely perceptible." He spoke in a monotone voiced difficult to hear over the horse's steps and his elevated position.

"An animal?" I noticed our pace was slowing. Elijah and the two other riders had moved ahead of our position leaving only Simon and myself to hear the testimony.

"It was tracking us. Tracking us for miles. I don't know of an animal that would track four men on horses. I would catch flashes of it moving through the brush on my flank. Quietly moving no more than twenty feet away." He was now sounding like someone telling a ghost story around a campfire.

"The others? Did they see anything?"

'We had spread out to cover more ground. Each rider responsible for a swath of forest stretching more than a 20 yards. Close enough to hear but not visible to one another through the thick tree cover. The noise of the other riders added to the creature being able to hide his whereabouts." The rider was noticeably sweating again as he relived the events.

Creature. Odd description given he had already shared he did not think it was an animal. 'You fired. Why? Were you threatened?"

He looked at Simon again. Simon smirked this time as if he didn't believe his fellow rider's story. "Go ahead. Tell the Sheriff what you saw."

He hesitated to share what he had seen as if to question his own story. "It charged at me. After all that time following me it charged for some reason. I had descended a ravine and was more isolated than ever from the others. It knocked into the back of my mare causing me to nearly fall off the startled horse. It ran off through the woods before stopping. I removed my shotgun and dismounted the horse. I stared towards the area where the noise had stopped. I secured my horse to a tree and took a few steps into a small clearing. Kneeling on my right knee, I scanned the area for any signs of the intruder."

His breaths were shortening as if he were physically back in the woods and under attack. I alternated looking at the rider and Simon. Simon continued to express his disbelief. I sensed the recounting of the story was taking a toll on the man. "I didn't get your name."

The question seemed to bring him out of the trance like state he was in. He looked directly at me as his breathing returned to a normal pattern. "Leroy Davis."

I nodded. The question served its purpose. He seemed centered again. "What happened next Mr. Davis?"

"It came at me. Zig zagging through the brush in its approach. I tried to aim but its erratic movements made it as impossible as grabbing a fish out of water with your hand. I fired into the brush before it knocked me to the ground. I gave a brief chase, but it had disappeared. Disappeared just as quickly as it had before." His breathing began laboring again.

I must say I was beginning to agree with Simon. The story seemed implausible at best. "Are you sure it wasn't an animal? A wolf protecting its den?"

He brought his horse to a stop. Simon continued up the path seemingly annoyed by the entire conversation. Reaching into his side pocket, Leroy retrieved a small piece of clothing. "This was torn away from whatever it was that attacked me." He handed the cloth over to me. It was only a few inches of a garment. "I've never known an animal to wear clothes." He kicked at his horse and caught up with the others ahead of me.

I turned the cloth over to inspect the other side. It appeared to be blood-stained. It wasn't even fully dried. Why didn't he show the others? He could have justified his story.

We made it to the church as the sun was beginning to set. Simon made each person available for me to interview. One by one they entered the church to be questioned. I turned and leaned over the pew to question each witness as they sat in the row behind me.

McElroy and Whitfield had little to add to what I had already discerned from talking to Ezekiel. The stories aligned. It seemed unlikely, from what I gathered, that they were involved in any way with the three-missing people.

It was Leroy who had new information to share. He sat down and placed his brimmed hat in his lap. His fingers nervously moving around the edges as he shifted it in a circular pattern. He was still shaken from the episode in the woods. His fragile state could help me extract his statement. If I comforted him, he might just give me something. He married into the Turner family. This gave him access to family secrets. He was both an insider and an outsider.

"Mr. Davis. How did you come to be part of the Divine Commune?" I removed my note pad and prepared to write.

"Please call me Leroy." I nodded. "I came to the area about thirty years ago. I was a trade worker. Looking for work. Found some in the area. I met Mr. Whitfield at the Town Diner. I didn't know anyone in town other than the family I was working for off Rehl Road. He introduced me to Simon. I joined the church shortly after." Having him talk about something so far in the past separated his thoughts from the recent events.

"You eventually married Simon's sister." I smiled acknowledging the joy a marriage usually brings to someone's life. "I guess you passed the test." I transitioned from a smile to a brief laugh to let him know the comment was in jest. He answered anyway.

"I felt like every day was judgment day." He looked around the empty church. "A twenty-year courtship. I must have finally earned Simon's approval." He forced a laugh of his own to reciprocate mine.

"Did Margaret and Jeremiah seem happy? You must have gotten to know them pretty well over the years."

Even though the church was silent, and no one had entered, he looked around again to confirm it was vacant. "As happy as any long-lasting marriage, I guess." He thought about how his answer might be received. "Wow, that sounded really cynical. What I mean is, they raised their two boys. And they're good boys. Both. In Gods eyes, they have raised two boys in faith. This is the primary reason we are tasked with as Christians, to keep the sacrament of marriage pure and to raise our kids to be dutiful Christians. True happiness comes when we are judged for our sins by our creator." He vacillated between his beliefs and those that were indoctrinated in him over the years.

He wasn't going to impugn Jeremiah. He was, after all, his brother-in-law through marriage. "Christine Ferguson. I know she lived with Jeremiah and Margaret. What can you tell me about her?"

Leroy looked through me. His eyes no longer seeing the person sitting in front of him. I sensed he had a deep connection to this woman. "I joined the church after Christine. From what I was told, she was a lost soul when she came to the Commune. Lost like many of us, in that we had not accepted the Lord, Jesus Christ, as our savior. The Turner's took her in just like they did me. The only difference is she had no other options. She was pregnant and had nowhere to turn. Except one." His eyes were getting glossy from an increasing amount of fluid build-up.

"She was pregnant?" Ezekiel had not shared that with me. It was both a question and an unintended response to his statement. It is best to slow down and think through each question to avoid falling into any traps.

Leroy proactively ran the sleeve of his arm across his eyes. It worked, at least momentarily, to delay tears from falling down his face. "She lost the baby during childbirth. She never seemed the same. Never seemed present after she lost the baby. Always appeared to be thinking of someone or somewhere else. We didn't talk much after her baby died."

I leaned in curious about this woman story. "The two of you talked while she was pregnant?"

The corners of Leroy's lips arched up ever so slightly. "Yes." He was reflecting on the conversations. They must have been meaningful to the both of them.

"Who was the father of the child?" I felt he would answer the question based on his previous responses.

Leroy shook his head. "I don't know. She never told me."

Dead end. "You mentioned somewhere else she could turn. Did you mean the church?"

There was no holding back the tears this time. The question triggered an extreme emotional response. His muscular physique giving way to a man undone by his actions. He shook as he placed his face between his hands with his elbows resting on his knees. The outburst filled the empty church. I looked around to see if it anyone from outside heard the commotion. None of the doors opened. We were still alone. The man across from me overwhelmed by something he had done in the past.

"Leroy. Whatever it is you have to say, she deserves for you to say it now." I prompted him to respond.

He continued to shake unable to control the wave of feelings rushing over him. I moved back and gave him time. He was guilty of something. Something that he has been holding in for a long, long time. I was at a loss for how to get him to answer. To divulge the information that was literally tearing him apart. I glanced around the church for inspiration. I saw the confessional booth in the corner of the facility. It was far from natural for me to bring religion into an investigative procedure. I knew he was a man of faith and I sensed he wanted absolution.

"Leroy." I said his name to try and garner his attention. His head remained down with his face buried in his hands. "We sit here in this place of worship. A place that should compel us to do what is right no matter how difficult it is for us to confess our sins. This burden can only be lifted by God. It can only be lifted if your answer leads to not only your salvation, but of those dear to us that our missing."

His head slowly rose from his hands. His face covered in the aftermath of his emotional outburst. He slogged his way through his confession. "Christine told me about her father. Charles." As he said his name, more tears gushed from his eyes. His hands still elevated and out in front of his face. Both shaking noticeably as if he could collapse again in shame. "She asked me to reach out to him in her time of need. To let him know she was okay." One hand wiped across his face leaving the residue all over his fingers. He looked at me for direction.

I sat in this church as an unqualified recipient of this man's penance. "Only the complete truth can put you on a path to redemption."

"I called her dad. I did as she asked." You could see the pain on his face. I didn't understand the reaction since he had done what she asked of him. "He answered." His face went immediately back into his hands. The tears returning to their previous level.

I didn't have to implore him anymore. He staggered to his feet using the pew to support his body weight. "O' God, please forgive me for me for my sins." He yelled out loud.

I place my hand on his, "how did you sin?" Still unsure of the reason for his guilt.

He softened his voice. "I lied. I went to Simon before seeing Christine. He said Christine needed this place. Needed to be free from all outside distractions. He said a life of faith was the only way she would find salvation. She had already given into temptation. I lied to her that day. I saw the hurt in her eyes. She believed her dad had died. And then, and then, the baby didn't make it. I was going to tell her hoping it would console her. Simon convinced me it was for the best if she stayed at the Commune. He said the church would fill the void."

He fell back into the pew causing a loud thud to emanate through the small church. I stood up and walked to the back leaving him to sulk on his own. I turned before exiting through the door to see him in the same position. I couldn't absolve him. It wasn't for me to decide his fate. In my opinion, he deserved the weight of the guilt he carried. He could have chosen to lift it years ago if he had just told the young woman.

Opening the church door allowed his cries to be heard by Simon. He reacted by moving quickly to meet me at the entrance.

"A grown man crying in my church. Only a Reverend should illicit such a response. I trust you are focusing on the right things Sheriff. The important matter at hand is the disappearance of my brother." He motioned with his head for Elijah to go into the church. It was undoubtedly to find out what Leroy had shared.

I dismissed their games. Their struggle to maintain a sense of power. It escaped them more and more as each day passed. Their church was dwindling, they had lost a brother, they needed outside help, and most of all, they had no answers.

Simon stood by my side observing the beauty of the grounds. Darkness had fallen on the Commune while I was questioning Leroy. "You should join us in the morning for a service to bless our ongoing search. I feel we are closing in on finding Jeremiah. The Lord has provided a possible place where we can find him."

Still looking out over the field I replied, "I think I'm good Reverend. I need to get to work early."

Simon turned to me and placed his hand on my shoulder. His touch nearly causing me to visibly shudder. "You mistake my invitation as a choice. If God is not in your heart than you will not find your way. You can stay in the Commune tonight. This will give you the extra time you need to include our creator in your schedule."

I never turned to him. It might compel me to punch his scrawny, pale face. "Thank you for the offer. I will take you up on both accounts. Before we call it a night. Can I see the cabin where your parents lived?"

"Good news Sheriff. I planned for you to sleep in the cabin. It is a bit rustic. Dad preferred it that way. Does that work for you?" His fingers tightened their hold on my shoulder.

I smiled still facing away from him. "That will be just fine."

Chapter 17: Collusion

Simon personally guided me to the cabin where his parents lived. He spoke very little as we made our trek. The past few days had clearly weakened him. He lit a couple of lanterns and placed them in the one room cabin. The light managed to stretch across most of the space. The walls were bare except for a crucifix hanging above the only bed.

Simon confirmed my attendance at the morning service and shut the door behind him. I turned completely around looking over every inch of the space. I noticed a small kitchen area in the corner. It had just a few cabinets and a sink. A loaf of sliced bread, cheese and a carafe of water were perched on top the counter. It had been hours since I had consumed anything.

I took the few steps it took to reach the counter. A note was left under the plate of cheese. "Grudge not one against another, brethren, lest ye be condemned: behold, the judge standeth before the door. Ye have lived in pleasure on the earth, and have been wanton; you have nourished your heart, as in the day of slaughter. Nourish your body tonight Sheriff, nourish your soul in the morning. Simon."

I crumpled the paper up in my hand and tossed it across the room. This food is going to do one thing.

It is going to be the fuel that allows me to bring you to justice.

After consuming every bit of the food offered, I examined the cabin carefully. I brought a lantern with me as I crawled across the floors on my hands and knees. I noticed a discoloration of the wooden flooring near the bed. It was a darkened area extending out in a non-uniform manner. It was impossible to determine the cause. It could have been stained by blood or from a spill. There was no way to know what caused it or when it may have happened. It had a weathered look indicating it had been there for some time.

The search of the cabin did not result in finding any significant evidence. Why did Ezekiel mention the cabin if it held no clues to the disappearance of his mom? The evidence in the workshop further confirmed Jeremiah's deviant behavior. What was this place supposed to expose?

I rested on the bed. As uncomfortable as it was, it was still a welcomed respite from a long day. The exhaustion I felt would typically result in me falling asleep quickly. Frustratingly, I stared up at the ceiling of the cabin knowing I had less than 18 hours. 18 hours before Sheriff Wagner would come to the Commune. This is the time that I had to find Margaret and Christine. The time I had to get concrete evidence incriminating Jeremiah and Simon of the crimes they have committed. The time I had to hopefully find a path to Laura. Resting seemed like an inconsequential activity with so many people counting on me. And yet, if I had no energy, I may not be able to fight when needed. I closed my eyes and pictured Laura. First, as the ten-year-old girl I rescued at the train trestle. Then, as the young adult who visited me at my house. She accomplished so much in 12 years. She graduated from college. The same broken and beaten child had persevered. She loved her mom and my friend, Jean Perry, the woman that adopted her. The thoughts swept over me and gave me a sense of comfort and inspiration at the same time.

My eyes remained closed as I drifted off to sleep.

I awoke suddenly when I heard a noise come from just outside the cabin. I had no idea how long I had slept. I cleared my eyes and quickly retrieved my gun. I grabbed a lantern and made my way to the door.

In times of uncertainty, always fall back on what is the most likely cause of the disturbance. It was part of my military training. The best guess is Simon or one of his men were coming for me. Perhaps Leroy was just as forthcoming with them as he had been with me. Maybe they got to Ezekiel too. There were plenty of reasons for them to act and act now before I discovered more incriminating evidence. Sheriff

Wagner said it himself, he warned me of the danger of investigating the Commune beyond Jeremiah's disappearance.

I blew out the lantern to hide my position. I crouched down behind the door and slowly pushed it open with the tip of my gun. A small opening between the wooden slat and the door frame allowed me to search the area for the cause of the disturbance. I extended the end of the gun out into the cool night air. The clear skies provided a soft blue aura of light emanating overhead from the nearly full moon.

I slowed my breathing and focused my thoughts. I may have to fire my sidearm and the chances of hitting the target will require a steady hand.

I saw a flash of white clothing move past a few trees not far from the cabin. My mind attempted to recreate the image in my head. I slowed it down as if I were looking at it frame by frame. It wasn't a man. Why would a woman be running through the woods at this hour? I questioned my own thoughts. Was I dreaming? Clear your head, you must be at your best.

I couldn't let it go. Whatever had flashed through the woods may be in danger. I broke from the cabin in a full run. The door slamming into the wood frame causing a loud crack to reverberate through the woods. I moved quickly to the tree line for cover. I hoped the chaos from my erratic burst from the cabin would protect my movements.

My approach must have startled the person hiding in the woods. They made it to their feet and began noisily maneuvering deeper into the brush. As I gave chase, the light from the moon became hidden by the thick foliage overhead. All I had to guide me were the sounds marking the location of the individual. They were unpredictable and loud but easy to identify the direction in which they were headed. The noise grew louder and more frantic as I closed in on them. Small branches whipped against my face as they returned to their natural position. I moved my arms up in front of me like a boxer to shield as many blows as possible. My legs were dragging the forest undergrowth with me prolonging the chase.

I reached out and felt the clothing covering the back of the individual. My hand separating and landing again as our movements jerked in every direction. I was able to grab a handful of material and pull. The action caused both of us to fall backwards to the ground. It was a dress that I had clutched in my hand. I could now see the long hair flowing over the back of the material. This confirmed the gender of the person fleeing the scene. She continued to fight to get free from my grasp. It was a futile attempt given her small stature. It gave me a minute to recover from the chase. She eventually stopped squirming and began yelling, "let me go, let me go."

I rolled on to my side and covered her mouth with my hand. "Quiet." The last thing I needed was to be found in the woods by Simon or one of his men. Inches apart, I was now able to see her face even in the darkness. The rapid breaths from her mouth landing on my neck. Her eyes moved down to my chest. They seemed fixated on my badge. "That's right. I am a police officer. My name is Conway. Are you hurt? Are you in danger?"

Her eyes opened wider as I spoke. Her breathing slowed and what little resistance she had maintained subsided.

"I am going to remove my hand. You cannot scream. I am not here to harm you." She moved her head up and down ever so slightly, enough for me to trust she would remain quiet.

I slowly removed my hand from her mouth and awaited her response. "I'm okay." Her accelerated breathing prevented her from continuing for a moment. "Christine."

I moved to my knees in shock at finding one of the alleged missing persons. "You're Christine. Christine Ferguson?"

She continued to nod her head as tears formed in her eyes. She smiled, "Yes. Yes."

I put my arm around her back and helped her to a seated position. "I didn't hurt you, did I?"

She moved her head side to side as she brushed off the remnants of the forest from her clothing.

I joined her in picking off a few leaves from her back and shoulders. "Where are you going?"

Her expression displayed her reluctance to tell me anything. We had just met. Why would she trust me?

"I want to show you something in the cabin. It is why I came back." She spoke calmly like a person on a mission. The chase would have rattled most individuals leaving them in distress or even shock. I've had soldiers in my command with less poise.

I nodded and helped her to her feet. We quietly trudged through the woods back to the cabin.

"I searched it. There is nothing in the cabin." I hoped the words were not disappointing for her to hear.

She kept walking as if I hadn't spoken. We reached the door and proceeded inside. I lit one of the lanterns and handed it to her. "Show me."

After grasping the lantern, she immediately turned to the kitchen. She walked slowly to the far-left cabinet.

Squatting, she placed the lantern on the floor. She looked up at me as she opened the door. Her hand disappeared into the cabinet along with half her upper body. She emerged with a stack of papers. My look had expressed the disbelief I felt over not finding the evidence. I took the lantern and wedged myself into the open cabinet. The letters had been concealed behind the back panel of the cabinet. Easily missed in a cursory search.

The cabinet door shut behind me as I moved back to the floor. Christine had moved to the bed and was now sitting in the dark. I brought the lantern with me as I made my way to her. Sitting beside her, she began to sort through the documents. I had so many questions to ask. I felt it best to let her continue. Afterall, she was sharing something that was important enough to hide.

She softly spoke as she referenced one of the papers. "Many of these were written by James Turner's wife. Like this one." She held one up to the light and read a section from it. "Hear, O heavens, and give ear, O earth: for the Lord hath spoken, I have nourished and brought up children, and they have rebelled against me." She lowered the letter to her lap while continuing to interpret its contents. "What son kills his father? What family preaches their spirituality while their actions conflict with everything they say? Jeremiah killed his dad. Mary knew it. The proof you need is captured here in her words."

She handed me half of the letters as she finished speaking. I clutched them between my two hands feeling the warmth of her skin as our flesh briefly overlapped. "What are those?" My eyes were fixated on the remaining pages still on her lap.

Christine looked down at them and smiled. "These are my words. My story. I am taking them with me. They are not Simon's or the Commune's to keep." She moved them to her chest placing both her hands across the front of them. "They belong to someone else now. Someone special to me."

I felt compelled to interrogate her as a witness and potential suspect. The civil servant in me wanted to secure all the papers she clung to as evidence. The weathered look of the woman beside me caused me to desist. She had given me what I needed. I put my arm around her and pulled her close to me. Her hold on the papers never diminished.

"I understand. You keep them. I suspect you have some knowledge of Margaret's and Jeremiah's disappearance?" I felt conflicted. I had to ask even though I recognize how much it appeared this woman had already endured.

She turned away from me to hide her face. She did know something. Something she was afraid to share.

Christine broke the silence with an inconvenient truth. "I must go. The sun will rise soon." Fear was written all over her as she stood up visibly shaking at the thought of being discovered.

I must have slept most of the night before Christine's scurrying had awakened me. I reached for her arm to prevent her from leaving the cabin. "I can't let you go Christine."

Her head started moving side to side in a hectic manner. She seemed in disbelief that I would restrain her.

"I can get you out of here. Safely. I promise." Reassuring her was going to be difficult given her previous reaction.

She collected herself and calmly responded. "No, you can't. Simon will stop you, or confront you if you try to leave with me. I have navigated in and out of these walls undetected more times than I care to remember. My best chance of escaping is for you to let me go."

It made some sense but letting her go would be a direct violation of my duties. And yet, I refrained from responding as I contemplated her request.

"You have to let me go. Please." She was still firmly grasping the letters against her chest with one hand.

I stared into her eyes and altered my plan. "You can get out unseen?" She nodded as her demeaner changed from fear to hope. "You have to meet me once you are outside of the walls. I can get to you after I attend the service in the church." I released her arm as I finished the sentence. Avoiding an unnecessary confrontation might be the best course of action.

"I will. On safe grounds. In the woods. I will. Thank you, Jack." She continued to stand in front of me even though the sunrise was beginning to slice through the darkness.

She was waiting for the rest of the plan. We needed a meeting place. A landmark. A place easy to find and well-hidden at the same time. "Meet me at 11am under the trestles. The south-end of the elevated track." I was still not sold she would keep her word. If she was involved in any way with the disappearance of Jeremiah or Margaret, she may decide to run. I attempted to hedge my bets just in case. "I have something to share with you as well. Something you will want to hear. The information came to me as part of my investigation. I know it will mean a lot to you."

Christine looked puzzled by the obscure statement. She nodded in compliance with every mannerism conveying she would follow through and meet me at the trestle. "I will tell you everything at the trestle. Jack, you don't have to take communion at the service. I stopped years ago. They never forced me. I couldn't stand the hypocrisy of taking communion from the very hands that have blood on them."

Her words were just as ambiguous as what I had expressed to her. As I thought about what she said she kneeled next to the bed. Lowering her head, she softy kissed the metal bed frame. She remained in the position for a few minutes as if she were praying. Christine stood in one motion and turned to the door without speaking. She peeked outside to make sure we were not being watched before racing out into the crisp morning air.

I thought about her movements. The moment of silence. She still believed in something. She kept her faith all this time. Why did she return to the cabin? The risk she took did not seem to justify the reward of having retrieved the letters.

Wait. She called me Jack. I never gave her my first name. I quickly moved to the door to see if she was still in sight. She knew more about me than I did about her. But how? Peering into the woods, I saw no sign of her movements. My eyes darted left as a horse and rider were approaching the cabin. I must give her some cover in case she had not made it out of the Commune. I ran out and met the horse bringing it to a sudden halt. Simon had ridden out to see me. I purposefully stood east of the colt, forcing Simon to look away from the woods.

"Good morning, Simon." I extended my arm for the perfunctory hand shake.

Simon clasped my hand in his and abruptly moved my hand up and down. "Good day, Sheriff. I trust the food and quarters were acceptable."

I smiled knowing small talk typically infuriated me, but in this case, it was providing Christine more time. "Your generosity is very much appreciated, and the accommodations were more than adequate."

"I came to remind you about the service. Our mass will begin in one hour. I trust you are still planning on attending?" Simon had a way of sounding condescending even when he wasn't trying to be.

I nodded. "Yes, sir. The rest did me good and I'm ready to get back to it."

"I also brought you some food and milk." He handed me a cloth bag and a closed jar with the milk. Simon stared at me for an uncomfortably long time before looking around the entire property from atop his horse. He kicked the side of the large beast and began to trot off. "One-hour Sheriff."

I searched the woods with my eyes again. Thankfully there were no signs of Christine.

I need to attend the service. It was the best way to reduce the chances of anyone knowing what I had discovered, a material witness with information likely to end the case. After mass, I will tell Simon I need to check in at the office. This will give me a window of time to rendezvous with Christine at the trestle. I'll take her statement and get her to the station. I'll bring everyone to the Commune. The time has come for the Turner family to pay for their transgressions.

I went back inside the cabin and sat on the edge of the bed. The letters from Mary Turner were still strewn about the top of the thin mattress. I had never heard this woman speak. The last time I was at the Commune, she was in a trance like state repeatedly striking her own head. It is an image that haunts me daily. Her voice was now being heard through the words in her letters. A mom losing control of her children. Desperate to instill the same Christian beliefs that had guided her and her husband their entire life. I now understand why this woman was so tormented. The devout husband she loved, taken from her by the boys she raised.

The letters must be kept hidden. They are a peek inside the walls of the Commune. An inside look at the evil that has filled this place ever since James' death. A vacuum of power creating the perfect storm for criminal behavior. No checks and balances. No judges or laws to conform to. Buoyed by a belief that all they do is for and through God. I don't know what will happen the day each of them takes their last breath. I only know their day of reckoning on earth is coming soon.

I returned the letters to the same place where they had been hidden for decades.

Chapter 18: Last Rites

I prepared for what could be an eventful day. My sidearm and shotgun loaded and ready if needed. The stakes have been raised since I set foot on the property of the Divine Commune. The likelihood of an altercation seemed imminent.

I finished the breakfast Simon had provided and made my way to the church. My investigation winding down. I had letters incriminating the Turner's. I have a statement forthcoming from a person of interest. I have less than eight hours before Sheriff Wagner takes over the operation. Unfortunately, I am wasting the next hour hearing Simon preach once again to his followers.

The church was coming into view as I strolled atop Moses into the clearing. The same few cars were parked in the field near my truck. The same people making their way into the church. Their movements seemingly rote and driven subconsciously. Did they ever stop and think about their actions? Who they were choosing to be the conduit between them and their faith?

Leroy was standing at the door of the church as I approached. His head was down with most of his face obscured by the brim of his hat. It failed to cover the noticeable marks on his jaw. He opened the door for me without ever looking up. I felt responsible for whatever they put him through. I had no idea if he shared the same details or not. It only heightened my already elevated sense of danger. I could be walking into a trap. Outnumbered and out armed with no way to secure back up. I walked in anyway.

I sat towards the back attempting to keep most of the congregation in front of me. If anything goes sideways, I want to give myself a fighting chance. Simon was already standing at the altar. He was dressed in his normal black pants, white button up shirt and black neckband. Two items were placed on the top of the altar. Simon was preparing for communion. He filled a chalice with wine before returning the cup to a cabinet on the side of the elevated platform. Next, he broke some bread into bite size pieces and placed them in a plain looking bowl.

I took the time to observe everyone seated in the church. I moved from person to person confirming they were present the day before. I accounted for everyone except Ezekiel. He was missing. I had seen the visible evidence inflicted on Leroy. I worried Ezekiel's fate might have been worse. His younger brother, Thomas, was sitting next to Elijah. His head was also down and avoiding any eye contact.

The church door opened behind me causing me to turn quickly while placing my hand on my sidearm. It was Leroy. He was finished with his task of ushering

in the church goers. He sat in the very back pew.
Yesterday, he was near the front. His location would
make it challenging for me to keep an eye on his
movements without being noticed. The whole affair
was unsettling.

My head returned to the altar as Simon began the
service. It was clear to me he always has a message
hidden in the scriptures he shared. Today was no
different. He was clearly calling out individuals that
had lost their faith. He referenced a wolf in sheep's
clothing. Maybe I was reading too much into it, but it
seemed directed at Leroy and perhaps Ezekiel.

Simon's voice filled the church as his rhetoric swelled.
"But he that is an hireling, and not the shepherd,
whose own the sheep are not, seeth the wolf coming,
and leaveth the sheep, and fleeth: and the wolf
catcheth them, and scattereth the sheep."

He continued with his own words, "we have a wolf in
our presence. A wolf trying to scatter our sheep. The
only way the wolf will find his way into the kingdom of
heaven is to ask for forgiveness for his sins."

Leroy stood behind me causing me to once again
grasp my sidearm. He made his way out of the pew
and slowly walked to the front of the church. Simon
watched each step of his deliberate walk to the altar.
Leroy fell to his knees on the first step beneath where
Simon stood.

Simon looked out over the congregation and locked onto my position. "Do we not have another wolf among us? Do we not have another tortured soul in need of redemption? In desperate need to be put on the path toward eternal salvation?" He continued to stare in my direction.

I didn't budge or flinch. I was not going to the front of the church again. It was unnerving enough having gone through the ceremony yesterday.

Simon seemed irritated that I did not react. He returned his focus to Leroy. "Remove your hat out of respect for the Lord."

I leaned forward in my pew.

Leroy gingerly removed his hat. There was a thin wire with barbs protruding from it wrapped around his head. Even from the back of the church, I could see the droplets of blood escaping under the pressure of each point.

Simon placed his hand on top of Leroy's head. His fingers added pressure pushing the ring deeper into his skin. Leroy lowered toward the floor before extending his arm to support his upper body.

I now had both of my elbows on top of the pew in front of me. I frantically went through options in my head. I cannot sit here and let this man be tortured for doing nothing more than sharing the truth.

Simon thundered away again interrupting my thoughts. "But he that shall blaspheme against the Holy Ghost hath never forgiveness, but is in danger of eternal damnation. For what sin do you seek atonement?"

Leroy softly whispered something that was not audible to most of us in the church.

Simon applied more pressure to the metal wire as indicated by the whites of his knuckles. "When you spoke your lies, you said them loud enough for God to hear. Let him hear your penance as well."

Leroy shouted out in a mix of what sounded like a scream and cry at the same time. "I lied!"

I placed my hand on my sidearm as drops of blood were now streaming down Leroy's face. I was readying to stand when Simon released his grasp. Leroy fell back off the stair to the floor of the church.

"Return to your seat. You will be allowed to take part in communion for having confessed your sin. May the body and blood of Jesus Christ wash over you and purify your soul." Simon walked down the few steps and removed the wiry crown from Leroy's head. It agitated the open wounds even more. Leroy went to replace his hat before Simon stopped his hand. "No. The hat stays in your hand. We all need to see the physical result of your sins. They are symbolic of the wounds we cannot see marking your soul. A soul that God will restore as you partake in his ultimate sacrifice."

Leroy staggered to his feet. He used each pew for support as he made his way back to his seat. I was astonished at what I had witnessed and that the others watched without acting. A few even shouted Amen and Alleluia during the whole ordeal.

I watched him lower himself on to the wooden seat. For the first time today, he looked me in the eye. The once proud and sturdy man broken down at the hands of Simon's henchmen.

I am thankful now that Christine is not behind these walls. I am grateful that she will soon be free of this place for good.

Simon once again diverted my attention from Leroy to the front of the church. He started preaching again as he blessed the bread and wine. I was in a fog unable to make out what he was saying. He may as well have been talking through a door or with one hand over his mouth. All I heard was a mumbled string of characters.

He lifted the bowl over his head and continued to speak. He lowered it to the altar and made a sign of the cross. He then consumed a piece of the bread.

My head was clearing. His words recognizable again.

He raised the chalice with the wine over his head and spoke. "I tell you the truth, unless you eat the flesh of the son of Man and drink his blood, you have no life in you." He lowered the chalice and repeated the sign of the cross. He lifted the container to his lips and drank. Simon picked up the bowl in one hand while holding the chalice in the other. He made his way out from behind the altar. He moved to the top of the stairs. He lifted both items over his head once again.

His stance began to shake. He seemed to be overtaken by something.

He spoke again but his words were difficult to discern. This time it wasn't my lack of focus.

"That by means of death." He fell to his knees spilling some of the contents of the chalice on his shirt. His words choppy and incoherent. "for redemption of transgwessions – sunder the fwurst tessament." The bowl dropped from his hands as several of the church members rushed to his side. The chalice tipped over causing a red stain to permeate the steps as it reached the floor.

I sat there paralyzed. Christine did not come back for only the letters. She came back to kill Simon. The patriarch of the family that had inflicted so much pain on her over the years.

Elijah grabbed my arm from the pew and pulled me up. "Help him."

I nodded still in a daze from all that had happened. The fear that I would not reach Christine given what she had set in motion hours ago. I moved to the altar and pushed my way into the circle of people that had gathered around Simon. His wife was crying over top of him. I gently pushed her back into the arms of one of her grown children.

I removed the neck band and opened his shirt by unclasping the first few buttons. Simon was regurgitating small amounts of the fluid as he choked with each breath. I turned him on his side to clear his airway. More fluid poured from his mouth. This time it contained a denser liquid. His blood mixed with the fluid and spilled from his lips. Several of the people surrounding me knelt and began to pray. I looked at each of them knowing there was little else I could do for him. I saw Leroy standing at the back of the church with his hat covering his head. He turned and walked out while everyone else had their attention on Simon.

Simon reached up and took my arm. He stared into my eyes. He pulled me close to him and whispered in my ear. "The Lord works in mysterious ways." His head fell back to the stair as a smile began to emerge. It didn't last long though. Another cough splattered blood and wine across his face. Those around me gasped at the violent convulsion that launched the fluids from his mouth.

He had taken his last breath. I shuffled away from him. His family and friends replaced my position by his side.

Chapter 19: My Story

I was grateful Jack let me leave the cabin. My plan could have easily been derailed had he tried to escort me out of the Divine Commune. I just hope it didn't increase the risk and danger he was facing. It was already at such a high level. The people he is investigating will fight if pushed into a corner.

Part of me felt I had let him down. I didn't warn Jack about the deadly concoction I brewed up in Jeremiah's workshop. He had no idea what he was walking into when he went to the service this morning. Laura spoke about the strength Jack displayed when he saved her at the trestle. She spoke of his loyalty and commitment to the rule of law. He would not want to be an accomplice to my crime. I on the other hand had a son to protect and lifetime of abuse to justify my actions. When Simon falls, the church and its followers will crumble. It will give the Sheriff the opportunity to escape the Commune.

At least that is what I am telling myself as I head back to the sanctuary. Jack is not the only one facing a significant challenge. I must prepare Billy and Laura for what may come our way. Elijah and the friends of the church will come after us. They know the location of the confrontation with Billy. A confrontation Billy initiated to protect us. A temporary distraction to move them away from the entrance of the cave.

I passed by the well and slid down the side of the hill to the covered entrance. A sense of calm came over me. This may be the last time I have to sneak out of the Divine Commune. Within hours, the police will raid the campus. There will be ample evidence of wrongdoing. The best part, it is all because of me. Perhaps Margaret taught me something when she fired that gun at her abusive husband. In some cases, you have no choice but to fight for yourself and your family. There is still one person that I must fight for and ensure her safety. It is time to get Laura back to her mom.

I covered the opening and made my descent to the sanctuary. The torch light once again unmasked the beauty of the underground world. I raced down the cavern to where Billy and Laura were now living. I stopped as I passed the boarded-up nook where Billy had lived as a child. It is now a tomb. The final resting place for Margaret. Maybe she will get a proper funeral once the Commune falls. Ezekiel and Thomas deserve to know what happened to their mom and to say goodbye.

I kissed two of my fingers and placed them on the wood board. "I did it, Margaret. I have forever protected my son from Simon." I slid my fingers down the board and pressed my body against the hard surface. I would give anything to embrace her once again. To dance in each other's arm knowing the weight of Simon's reign was ending. I stitched together memories of her laughing from the precious moments we shared through the years. I tapped the board with my open hand a couple of times and retreated further down the cavern.

Tears of joy and sadness expressed my mixed emotions. I wiped them away to hide the events of the last few hours from Billy and Laura. The two of them have been through more than enough to last generations. It is time for them to have some peace.

I stepped into the opening and saw Laura sitting cross legged with her back to me. She was hunched over and rocking back and forth ever so slowly. She didn't notice I had stepped into the room. I quietly approached her from behind and saw she was writing in a journal. Laura turned as the heat of the torch warmed the air around her. "You came back."

I placed the torch in a crevice and fell to my knees beside her. I wrapped my arm around her and pulled her close. "We have to finish the story. Together."

Laura smiled and flipped through all the pages she had added since we last spoke. It was evident she filled the time nervously completing the stories I had shared. She flipped another page to an illustration. It was an amazing drawing of me in a beautiful gown. My fingers traced the image as I gently kissed Laura on her forehead. "Thank you. I have no pictures of myself. You have given me something better. You have captured my essence in a way a photograph could never do."

Laura's hand landed on top of mine as she squeezed it acknowledging my appreciation.

"I have something to add to the story." I reached under my arm and pulled out the letters from the cabin. Laura's eyes widened with excitement. "I have the words describing everything since I came to the Commune. Details that even I had forgotten over the years."

She sheepishly asked, "Is it okay if I read your letters?"

I smiled and replied, "You were right. It's not just my story. It's Billy's. It's just as much yours. And, yes you have my blessing to read them all." I handed them to Laura. "Where is Billy?"

Laura shrugged her shoulders as her face lost the joy it had just displayed. "He left early. He awoke and realized you were gone. He thrashed around so much he woke me a couple of hours ago. He mentioned the patrols and was concerned for your safety. I have been writing ever since trying to avoid thinking about what might have happened to both of you."

I had to keep my activities a secret from the two of them. It sounded crazy to me when I thought about it. Sneak back into the Commune. Poison the wine. Collect my letters and return unnoticed. They would never have allowed me to go. "I'm sorry Laura. I'm sorry I put you through that. Billy will be fine. You saw how he bounced back from his injury. You know how he can hide within feet of us and we never even know he is there." I smiled reflecting on the skills my son developed out of necessity. Skills that benefit him everyday in the woods.

"I know." Laura dropped to the blanket and rolled on to her back. Her fingers interlocking with the journal. The letters safely secured under them. "I still worry about him though. I always have. It's why I came back to the house on Pope Lick Road five years ago. It was never the house. It was him. It was his essence. This being that sacrificed everything for me only to see it taken away from him. I didn't know it then, but it is clear to me now."

I laid down beside her in the position the two of us had found to be very comforting the past couple of days. "Laura, this is going to be hard for you to hear. It is just as difficult for me to say." I saw Laura close her eyes as if she could shut out what I was about to share. Her mind unable to process any more pain. "It's time for you to leave this place. Leave for good and never come back. The Sheriff you admire so much is planning to meet me under the south end of the trestle at 11am. Except, Jack is not going to meet me. He is going to meet you. Billy is no longer your responsibility. He has me and I have him. I love you so much for all you have done for my son. But he cannot give you what you deserve. My story is detailed on the pages you are now holding. I don't want it to be your story in twenty years. We are kindred spirits, but your spirit has a lot of life left in it."

A few tears had found their way out of Laura's eyes even though they remained closed. She was moving her head side to side in defiance of what I had asked of her.

I placed my hand on the side of her face and moved it to mine. Her eyes blinked several times before opening under a glossy covering. "Your mom deserves to see you again."

Laura had become immersed with the idea that she had to be there for Billy. So much so, she had blocked some very special people out of her thoughts. She was consumed with keeping Billy safe and too afraid to leave him all alone.
It was evident Laura was now thinking of her mom. More tears flowed from her eyes. She needs to unburden herself of Billy. She can leave him to me now. I pushed up on to my knees and took both of Laura's hands in mine. I leaned over and looked her in the eyes. "There is a hole in me that will never be filled. The hole is all the minutes I missed holding my

son. I didn't know if he was safe. I didn't know if he was happy or even alive. I wouldn't see him for days or even years as Billy grew older. Every second like a missed heartbeat. I was never at peace with how things turned out. Until now. I can now be here full-time for my son. Your mom needs the peace of mind of knowing her daughter will be okay." I repositioned myself next to her to console Laura as much as I could.

Laura began crying openly as she turned on her side and put her arm around me. The letters and journal wedged between the two us. Her head was moving up and down acknowledging the thought of seeing her mom again.

As Laura cleared her head and her heart of everything that had built up inside of her I turned on my back.

Standing over the two of us stood Billy.

Shadows from the torch made it appear he was moving even though he was standing completely still. Remnants of his own tears had matted the wiry facial hair on his jaw. Laura became aware of my change in breathing. Her head turned from my shoulder allowing her to see Billy.

I contemplated what I could say. How much did he hear? It was difficult to explain complicated matters to Billy. To him everything was so much smaller, so much simpler. You love the people that love you. You protect them at all cost. You defend them from those that try to harm them. It was all extremes for Billy. There was no gray area in his world. I fault myself for not instilling in him a more flexible perspective.

"Billy..." He cut me off before I could say another word.

He remained standing over the two of us. He spoke in an understated tone, "no one leave."

I took another step back as the cries intensified. The church filled with wails from Simon's family and friends.

No more time could be bought. I had just witnessed a murder. Hell might break loose once the shock wears off. I needed to get reinforcements to the Commune. I turned from the altar to report the incident to the Sheriff.

"Where do you think you are going?" I stopped in my tracks as Elijah called out.

My back was to him. I had no idea if he was armed or not. "I have to report this to the Sheriff."

"You're the Sheriff." I heard his footsteps approaching from behind and the unmistakable feel of a double barrel shotgun pressed into my back. I exhaled knowing I had few options to escape.

"Your brother needs medical attention." I said it loud enough for everyone in the church to hear.

The end of the gun pushed against my back forcing me to take a couple of steps forward. "My brother is dead." I heard the hammer of the gun being cocked.

"You're right Elijah. Simon is dead." No since disputing the obvious. My only chance was to rattle him. He was already emotional. I had to push him. "You going to shoot me in his place of worship."

The gun struck my back again forcing me to take a few more steps. He was ushering me towards the door. I guess shooting a man in an open field is far less damning than in a church.

Elijah's wife hollered out, "what are you doing Elijah?" The words shocked me. Someone with enough courage to confront this man. I tried to look over my shoulder to see his reaction.

His eyes never left my position as he responded. "This does not concern you. Tend to Anne and the children." He continued to move me towards the door of the church.

"I didn't kill Simon." I voiced it in a stern tone. "All you outsiders killed him. You brought evil to our Commune. You took away our spiritual leader. You took away our brother. Simon might have found it in him to forgive. I'm not Simon." We reached the door of the church.

I took a deep breath. I may have let Christine down. I should have pulled my gun as soon as Simon dropped to the floor. If I go down, the letters could remain concealed. Justice will not prevail.

I pushed the door open under duress. It swung freely as a blast of light filled the area. I stepped down with Elijah still trailing me closely.

"Time for your judgment day Sheriff." The end of the gun moved up my back and was now pressed against my head.

I closed my eyes. I pictured Laura. I whispered, "I'm sorry".

The metal end of the gun abruptly left my head as a loud thud proceeded Elijah dropping to the ground. I rolled to the side and unsheathed my sidearm.

Standing over Elijah's fallen body was Leroy. The butt of his gun held firmly in his left hand. He kicked the shotgun away from Elijah and took a handkerchief from his pocket. He wiped the new streams of blood from his forehead. They had managed to escape under the brim of his hat. "Consider yourself to be judged not guilty." He smirked as I crawled over to Elijah.

I gave him a nod as I secured handcuffs around Elijah's wrist. "Get out of here. You can come back once the smoke clears."

Leroy had a look of a man that had exorcised his demons. A relief that was hard to put into words. He began to move to his vehicle when I stood up and stopped his progress.

"Christine is alive. I spoke to her last night. I know what the Commune has done to her. She will be safe soon." They were words he had earned the right to hear.

He closed his eyes briefly and tipped his hat in my direction. He turned without saying another word. I watched as he drove away from the Commune.

I ran to my truck leaving Elijah face down in the field with his wrists cuffed behind him. I hopped in the cab and began shouting on the radio. "Sheriff, do you read me? We have a 10-64 at the Divine Commune. Over."
"Jack, what the hell is going on?" The Sheriff's voice came piercing through the radio.

I pressed the call button and replied, "Simon Turner is dead. I witnessed it. Probable cause is poison. Over."
I turned over the engine of my truck and began backing up. The members of the church were now filing outside to see what was happening.

"Dead?" The Sheriff paused, "Are you in danger, over."

My truck whipped sideways and kicked up a cloud of dirt. The pedal fully pressed against the floor board of the truck. I came to a stop and shifted into drive. I lowered my window and pointed my sidearm in the air. I clicked the radio so the Sheriff could hear my words. I screamed across the field towards the church. "All of you need to go back in the church and wait for the authorities to arrive." There was little movement from the church members. McElroy and Whitfield had their shotguns held against their chest. I fired my gun twice into the air. The shots caused the congregation to scatter. Most returned inside the doors of the church. A few, including the two-armed men, took cover behind some trees.

I wanted the Sheriff to hear everything before I released the call button. His response was not surprising given the chaotic nature of the call. "Jack! Gun shots. Are you hit?"

I pressed the pedal down to the floor again causing the tires to spin in place before gaining traction. "I'm not hit. I fired. At least two men are carrying guns. Maybe others. I must check on something. Over." I threw the radio on to the passenger seat as the steering wheel required the use of both hands.

The Sheriff was screaming over the radio in a rant filled with coarse language and demands. He was screaming at the other deputies to scramble as he alternated the targets of his vitriol.

I checked my rearview and none of the church members had moved. Elijah was still lying face down in the field. I didn't like leaving the scene without securing it first. However, if I stayed until the Sheriff arrived, I would compromise the safety of the material witness. Wags continued his verbal assault on the radio as I made my way through the tree-lined road to exit the Commune. I heard the sirens firing up in the background on each of his calls. They were already on the road and should arrive within minutes.

I turned the radio down as I approached the perimeter barricade around the Commune. The speedometer reached 60 mph as I crashed through the wooden gate. Splinters of wood flew in every direction. I turned the wheel to the side causing the truck to spinout. The side road around the outside of the fenced property line was now in front of me. It was the quickest way to get to the trestle. The road eventually runs parallel with the train tracks. The same tracks that lead to the trestle. The clock on the dashboard of the truck displayed the time. 10:15am. I have 45 minutes before Christine will meet me at the trestle. 45 minutes to figure out what to do when I have her in my custody.

Chapter 21: Condemnation and Salvation

"Billy. You have to listen to me." I tried my best to console him, but his anger was written all over his face. He felt betrayed by the only two people he thought loved him. He pushed me away as I tried to put my arm around him. It was a strong thrust that sent me flailing across the cave. I fell over Laura as I attempted to slow my momentum.

We huddled together unsure of what Billy might do next. He had his back to us and was fumbling with something. I had no idea how to comfort him. I'm not even sure it was possible given all the emotions he must be processing. He feared being abandoned more than anything in this world.

Billy turned to face us. The anger had dissipated from his expression. He appeared stoic in his demeanor. He was holding a lengthy rope in his hands. The threads, covered with sporadic blotches of blood, were woven together for strength. It was the dried blood from both Jeremiah and Margaret.

Laura's face was now pressed into my shoulder. She wanted shelter. A safe harbor from the storm that was brewing inside Billy. He knew I encouraged Laura to leave. This meant leaving him. Neither of us could explain this to him. He would never understand how leaving would be the best thing for Laura. The logic would be lost on his childlike mind.

Billy moved in as I put my arms completely around her. I wasn't going to let him harm her. He began moving the rope over and around Laura's limbs. He was attempting to restrain her in the same manner as when Jeremiah bound me in the sanctuary. Laura would let out stifled moans as he pulled and tugged on the loose ends of the rope.

He then turned his efforts to me. I tried again to talk to him. "Billy..." My words were stopped as he slapped his hand across my face. Laura winced having been conditioned to do so from when she was a child. He had never physically harmed me in all these years. The pain from the soft blow was dwarfed by the realization that my son had changed.

Billy continued the process of securing the two of us. He never made eye contact with me as he maneuvered around my body. I know he didn't have a plan. There is no way he could keep us restrained forever. He just hadn't had time to think it through to its conclusion. This was not going to bring him closer to Laura. He knows how Laura felt about her abusive birth mom. Billy killed her to protect Laura. Would he recognize his actions today to be the same?
Billy finished wrapping the rope and tightly tied off the end. He had successfully restricted our arms and legs from having any freedom of movement.

He began inspecting the letters that were now strewn about the two of us. I knew he couldn't read many of the words, but it didn't stop him from acting as if he was going over them line by line. He would look up at me after each one and shake his head. Each letter seemingly increasing the disappointment he associated with me.

He extended one letter over the flame coming from the candle. Billy let it drop from his hand as the fire quickly consumed the paper. The charred embers floated high in the underground cavern. A part of my story vanished from existence. He finished looking at another letter and brought it close to the flame. I remained completely still. I gave him no visible emotional response. He wanted me to be hurt. He wanted me to feel the same inside as he did. My lack of reaction caused him to crumple the paper up and throw it across the room.

"Must patwol the woods." I don't think he knew what to do. How to undo what he had already done. Patrolling the woods gave him a sense of purpose. It was something he was good at and it was ultimately to protect the two of us from harm. In his way, it may be his way of apologizing.

I had no way to protect myself should my words provoke another physical response from Billy. Still, I attempted to console him one more time. "Billy. I killed the leader of the bad men last night. I did it for you. I did it for Laura. They are not coming. There is no evil left outside of this cave. There is no one else looking for us." Billy remained a few feet away. The words did not incite the same level of anger as moments earlier. Yet he looked unsure of the sincerity of my words.

He scrambled over to the crumpled piece of paper he had tossed across the room. The quick movement startled both of us. We relaxed ever so slightly as we realized we were not the target. He crawled on all fours back to the candle and began spreading the paper back to its original form. He looked down a few lines and spoke. "I should have ended my baby's life." Laura looked up at me for the first time as Billy finished talking.

Unlike before, I could not contain my emotions. My arms pressed against the rope as I attempted to hide my face in shame. A few tears began streaming down from my eyes. I had to hear my son read those extremely painful words. Words a mom would never want their child to see or hear. Words written by a young woman that saw no hope or future for their child. I knew the pain he would endure over the course of his life. I knew Simon and his brothers would expose him to a world of evil and sin. It was the darkest of dark times for me. Billy was only six months old. My twice a day visits found him in his own filth and crying uncontrollably. As soon as I had him clean and fed, I had to leave him again. There is nothing I can say to ease his pain. "Billy, let me read the rest of the letter to you. Please." I knew the words. I knew every one of them. He wouldn't believe me though unless I showed him. "Please."

Billy slowly crawled next to the two of us and placed the letter on my outstretched legs.

"Remember how you moved your finger under the words when I read to you." Billy nodded and placed his finger immediately after the word life. "Move your finger as I read the words to you." Billy's finger began to slide across the paper as I read each word to him. Laura was now reading softly in unison with my voice. "The choices I have are limited. Whatever I decide, the consequences will be excruciating."

Billy's finger stopped. It is what I told him to do when he didn't understand the meaning. I looked at him in the eyes and said, "painful. Anything I chose to do would be painful." His finger continued to move forward after the sentence made sense to him. "If I take his life, I will also take mine."

Billy stopped again but this time I knew he understood the words. "You die with me?"

"Yes, Billy. I could not live without you." My eyes returned to the paper. "Let's finish the letter Billy." His finger moved slower under the weight of the words he was hearing.

"I will love my child. I will fill the emptiness in his life with love I have for him." I noticed a tear fall from Billy's eyes as I continued reading. His finger was now shaking as it moved along the lines of text. "His life is a gift. A gift that has been given to me when I needed it most. A purpose. A reason to move forward. I hope someday you will understand and love me for the sacrifices I have made to raise you. Love always, your mommy."

I dropped my head to Laura's shoulder. The only thing she could do to show support was rest her head against mine. Billy was still staring at the letter. A few drops from his eyes splashed on the page causing the ink to smear. He turned and moved to the entrance of the hidden underground room. He let the letter fall from his hand as he ran out of the space. It was too much for him. There was no way to know how he will act when he returns. Will he be angry or understanding? Will he harm us or let Laura go?

Jack Conway. Laura needs to get to Jack. We don't have long until the arranged meeting time at the trestle. "Laura, we have to work to get free. You are going to meet Jack at the trestle."

Laura looked me in the eyes and affirmed the plan. We both began to wiggle free of the restraints. We tumbled over several times as we fought to escape. Each time landing on the thin blanket that was covering the hard surface beneath it. Each blow, bruising and hurtful.

"Stop." I commanded Laura to stop moving. "This isn't working. He has us bound too tightly to break free. Our only chance to is to move together to the supplies on the other side of the room. We have to hope that Billy has left the scissors in his haste to leave."

We began the awkward journey towards the supplies. Each of us rolling over the other as we twisted our way a few feet at a time. Off the blanket, blunt edges from the eroded rock now met each fall. The rope absorbed some of the impact with the rest sustained by our exposed skin. We were grunting and groaning with each move. I went over the top of Laura again trying my best to not injure her in the process. The momentum threw me more forcefully this time towards the ground. My left wrist flexed to soften the jolt. My weight came down bending it backwards an unnatural amount. A crack echoed through the cavern as the bone succumbed to the force. I screamed out from the intense pain as I tried to shift the pressure off the joint.

Laura yelled out, "Christine!" She was helpless to do anything else. We were both lying face down, side by side.

I bit my lower lip and turned my head towards Laura. I cannot let her see the pain I am in. "We have to keep going. You need to roll over me again."

Laura knew the extra weight would only add to my pain. She hesitated as the side of her face was pressed against the cold rock.

I have never felt more intensity in my life than in that moment. Laura could see the determination on my face. I said one word and I said it confidently, "MOVE!"

Laura rolled her body against my side and onto my back. The weight pushed my hips down smashing my left arm between my body and the surface below me. The broken bone impinged even more from the previous fall. I did not scream out as before. I had to keep Laura moving and not thinking of me.

The weight lifted ever so slightly as Laura began to fall off the right side of my body. She landed on her back. We would have to repeat the movements several more times to reach the supplies. Dizziness clouded my head as the pain emanating from my wrist intensified. My left hand was useless now as it flopped around with each turn.

Our faces were covered in a slimy film from the journey. Laura spoke. "We've made it!"

I let out a sigh knowing the worst was over. "We need to work together to sit up." Minutes passed as we leveraged our bodies together to push up off the floor of the cave. We both let out a deep breath from all the energy it required.

Laura began to search around with her fingers. Her wrists were pinned to her body just like mine. She had a limited range of motion given how tightly the rope was secured around her arms.

We shuffled to the right in unison to uncover more items that were out of reach. Our bottoms would lift up and launch together before slamming back into the surface.

Laura pulled a bag to her side and began working on the rope drawstring that bound it together at the top. She only had one hand given her other one was pinned against the other side of her body. Frantically, she maneuvered her fingers in and out of the loops trying to loosen the string.

I placed my head against the side of the cave that was now behind us. I had no idea how much time had lapsed and if Laura would have any chance of making it to the trestle on time. We still had to free ourselves, climb out of the cave and make the mile or so jaunt to the location. We had to do all this, and hope Billy doesn't return. If he did, he would rightfully lose any remaining trust he had in either of us. He would deem us to be conspirators. Traitors that he would subject to whatever punishment he felt was justified. He will do all of this in a fit of rage that I fear he cannot control.

Laura worked the bag to an open position and pushed her hand inside. She clanged the items together as she groped the contents. One by one she pulled items out to make the search easier. She tossed utensil after utensil to the side. Even the knives were too dull to have any effect on the rope.

Her hand stopped moving in the bag. "What? What is it?" I leaned over her side to see what she had found.

Her hand slid out of the bag exposing a pocketknife. "I've seen this before. This is my knife. I used it to fight off Tommy at the train trestle. Billy must have retrieved it." She began the awkward fight to open the knife with only one hand. It slid around in her lap as she tried to maneuver the blade from the compartment. Her hands were covered in the wet substance from the cave floor adding to the challenge.

Finally, I heard the click of the blade as it sprung from the enclosure. Laura began to saw at the rope just above the knot tied at her side. Thread by thread broke away as she pulled the blade back and forth across the rope.

My head turned to the entrance. Please give us a few more minutes before he returns. Please. I stared intently into the blackness hoping nothing would appear. I could hear the slashing sounds coming from Laura's efforts to free herself.

She was yelling out, "C'mon. C'mon. C'mon." It grew louder each time. She knew time was ticking away on any chance she had to return to her mom.

I heard her laugh. It brought my head back to her. The rope relinquished its grip on her waist. She was feverishly weaving it in and out releasing more of her body with each pull. She got to her feet and pushed the remaining loops over her shoes.

She moved to me and began trying to untie the knot. It wasn't budging. "Laura. Look at me. Leave. Go to the trestle. Get to your mom." I said it calmly fully aware what the outcome would be when Billy returned.

Laura looked incredulous. "Not a chance." She retrieved the knife and began the same sawing action that freed her moments ago. A tear rolled down my face as I feared she would have the same fate as me if she stayed any longer.

I turned to the entrance again staring into the darkness. Please. Give her a chance.

My emotions lifted when I felt the rope loosen around my waist. My injured hand fell to the surface causing more pain to seep through my body. The condition of my wrist made it very unlikely I could climb out of the cavern. I had tried many times before when I was much healthier and could not make it.

Laura was almost finished unwrapping me. She looked at me. "I couldn't have done this without you." I fell into her as the rope dropped to the floor. She picked me up in one motion landing me on my feet.

We made our way to the entrance and into the darkness. Our progress impeded as we bumped into something. Billy. He had come back. Or maybe never left. If he was testing us, we failed him again. He pushed us both back into the room. We fell to the floor as he paced side to side. If he didn't know what to do before he was even more conflicted now. I pulled Laura to me and whispered in her ear. "Give me the knife". Billy was still pacing not looking at either of us. Laura shook her head side to side. She still could not bring herself to see Billy harmed.

"Give me the knife." The second request was honored. She discretely placed it in my right hand.

I stood up. Billy stopped pacing. His side to me, still facing forward. He did not acknowledge me but was aware of my movement.

"Son, it is time to do the right thing." I kept the knife by my side out of his view.

His head slowly turned towards me. "You not mawma anymowe. I not you son anymowe. My mawma left me in a cave to die."

His resolve showed in his stance. Neither of us were leaving without a fight. I raised the knife into the air. "You let her go. NOW!"

I could hear Laura's cries coming from behind me. It reminded me of why I must go through with the plan. I must give her the chance to get to Jack.

I lunged toward Billy and yelled to Laura, "RUN!" Billy easily stopped my arm as it swung forward. He squeezed my arm so hard the knife fell to the ground. He threw me down and jumped on top of me. My eyes found Laura still sitting behind me. Her head in her hands crying uncontrollably. Billy reached for the knife and lifted it up over his head. He placed it between both of his hands as he stared into my eyes. I mouthed the words, "I love you."

As he brought the knife forward, he fell off to the side of me. Laura was standing over me with a pan in her hand. I turned to Billy to see blood oozing from the newly inflicted wound on the side of his head. Laura reached out to me and lifted me off the ground. We both shuffled to the entrance as Billy struggled to get to his feet.

We moved into the darkness of cave. I fell into Laura with all of my body weight. Billy had a hold of my dress and was pulling both of us back to him.

Laura screamed, "NO!", as she could see what was coming behind me.

An extreme pain emanated from my shoulder. The knife remained pressed against my flesh as Billy kept his grip on the handle. "GO!" I yelled at Laura again.

I felt the blade being pulled from my flesh as Billy removed it from the wound. I turned and threw myself into him before he could thrust the knife again. I yelled for Laura to leave as a I struggled to stay on top of Billy. I had to give her a head start. Enough time to beat Billy to the trestle.

I was dismayed to see Laura's feet moving beside me. Billy eventually flipped positions and was overtop of me once again. Laura standing beside him with the pot back in her hand. I continued to fight Billy to distract him from her movements. This time she took a full swing knocking Billy unconscious with the powerful blow. He fell on top of me with the knife piercing my abdomen. I gasped as the pain from both wounds spread.

Laura nudged Billy off to the side of where I was positioned. I smiled at the courage she showed. The will to fight for both of us. "Laura. You must go. Tie Billy up. Leave the knife with me. You can still make it to trestle."

She placed the knife in my right hand and went quickly to tie Billy up with the rope.

"I want you to go with me." Laura returned to my side with tears flowing down from her eyes.

"I know. And you can take me with you. You can take my story. I should stay with Billy. Turn left into the tunnel. Go about 30 paces and take the right opening. It's a long crawl from there but you will see light. You'll know what to do from there. You will be in the woods." I didn't have much longer and there was no way Laura could get me out of the caverns. She knew it as well. My fate was sealed, and it was a fate I saw coming for a long time. To die with my son by my side.

Laura nodded and scurried around collecting all the journals and letters. She placed them in a bag and kneeled next to Billy. "I am sorry I couldn't do more for you. Thank you for protecting me." She moved to me and kissed my forehead. "You will be remembered. I will always remember what you have done. Your story will be told."

I smiled at Laura again letting her know it was okay to leave. She turned and disappeared into the darkness headed toward her salvation.

Chapter 22: Emergence

I wiped away the tears as I crawled through the cavern in search of the exit. I blocked Christine and Billy from my mind. Seeing my mom is my focus now. She is the reason it is time to leave this place. My heart already picking up its pace at the thought of holding her again.

My hands were not visible even inches in front of my face. I counted each move to gauge where to turn. The wall to the right fell away into an empty void. The opening matched the estimate Christine had described. It made sense now more than ever how this place could stay hidden all these years. How the bad men Billy spoke of missed the underground network of caverns. Any of the channels easily missed if you didn't know exactly what you were looking for.

I slithered my way along while carrying the bag containing Christina's letters and journal. I felt a pool of water as I stretched out to move forward. Cautiously, I proceeded not knowing the depth of the water I was about to traverse. I pushed the bag against the ceiling of the cave to keep it dry. The cave became that much colder as my body waded into the depression. My pants and shirt soaking up the frigid liquid. My teeth tapping together as my whole body shuddered. The water never got deeper than a few inches. Still, it cloaked most of my body in moisture. I crawled out of the water with my clothes clinging to my body.

The extra weight added to the challenge of lifting and pulling forward. My muscles weakening from the convulsions triggered by the coldness. The chill trapped against my flesh insulated by the saturated cotton fibers.

I was adjusting to the new temperature when I reached a second pool of water. This one shallower than the first but just as bone chilling. My breath escaping me as I quickly scrambled through it like a salamander. I stopped and placed my head on the bag. The cold rock pressing against the entire front of my body. I was still and so was the cave. There was no sound.   No dripping water to distract me from the reality of where I am.

Doubts started penetrating my thoughts. Did I take the wrong cavern? Would I ever make it out of this place? I continued crawling wondering if the light would ever come. I trudged along like a slug for ten more minutes.

The complete darkness started playing tricks on my eyes. It was very disorienting. I began seeing flashes. Flashes of light and quick glimpses of memories from the past. Images of me running through the woods as a child. Luke comforting me after learning of my abuse. Tommy forcing him out on the trestle and me following behind. The train relentlessly bearing down on me. I could feel the rocky surface vibrating beneath me as I thought of the power of the iron horse. I remember turning to see the light. The contrast with the dark blinded me leaving only a burned image of a ring of fire in my mind. Flashes of me running forward on the tracks as my eyes regained their clarity. Billy standing at the end of the trestle with his arms open.

His image replaced by a foggy light beginning to appear. It wasn't too far ahead. It seemed angelic. I picked up my pace as the light grew brighter. I began to be able to make out the sides of the cavern as the light found its way to my fingertips. I stretched out and saw my arm for the first time since leaving Billy's home. I know it wasn't any warmer than before, but I felt the same sensation as if it were directly exposed to the sun.

I shuffled a few more times and crawled out into an opening. The light was all around me now. I used the side of the cave to prop myself up on my feet. I remained lunged over in a squatting position hoping my strength would return. I looked up to see the climb that separated me from the woods.

The opening was about 15 feet overhead. The walls mostly smooth from the water that entered the cave. It left only a few edges. This was going to take any remaining strength that I had within me. I tied the drawstring of the bag around my waist to free my hands for the climb.

A few quick attempts landed me back on the floor as the path quickly dissipated. I chose another route and began the climb again. Christine was right. There was no way she could have made it. I thought about her as I made my way up the wall. A mom forced to make the ultimate sacrifice. I pictured her lying peacefully next to her son. The two of them taking their last breath together. A tear fell from my eye knowing she did it for me. Another tear fell for Billy. The boy who protected me all those years.

I reached high grabbing on to a small ledge and pulled up. My leg scurrying to find a foothold to take the pressure away off my arm. Miraculously, it landed on an edge big enough to hold my foot. I pushed up bringing me only inches from the top. The warmth of the sun was now surrounding me.

I reached for the edge. My fingers felt the dirt and grass that lined the entrance to the cave. One more pull and I should be able to thrust myself out of the cavern. I closed my eyes to summon the strength I would need. My effort delayed at the sound of footsteps coming from above.

"We have to be close."

Whoever it was, they were close enough for me to understand every word. I froze. Billy was right. They were coming.

"It was right around here. I know it. I know what I saw."

I slowly slid my hand back inside the cave opening, clinging to the wall and hoping to go unnoticed.

"We don't even know if my mom is out here. We should go back Leroy. The people back at the Commune can help us."

The Commune. No one at the Commune can be trusted. Christine made that very clear. The footsteps were moving all around me. How could they not see the opening? I felt like they were close enough to fall in at any moment.

"Well, whatever I saw, it cannot just disappear into thin air. Ezekiel there has to be some explanation."

I heard the footsteps separating. One moving further away and one moving even closer. My arms were losing the capacity to hold on. They were shaking uncontrollably. The intense fear I was feeling only added to my fatigue. I started slipping. I began scratching and clawing at the wall to maintain my position. A fall from this height could be debilitating.

My movements came to a sudden stop when I felt a hand grab my wrist. My body went limp. My feet sliding off the rocky surface. The person above me was now the only reason I wasn't falling to the bottom. I dangled perilously above the rocky floor. I looked up only to see light. The brightness not unlike taking a quick glance at the son when you were a child.

I began being pulled out of the cave.

"Ezekiel! Come back, I found someone."

I heard the noises of a second person approaching. They were grunting as the two were now joined in pulling me out of the cavern.

I slid over the edge as they both fell to the ground. My arm aching from the force used to pull me to safety. The angst I felt returned as I awaited their next action.

They both moved to my side. The man that pulled me out spoke first. "Are you okay?"

The words barely registered in my head. Subconsciously, I nodded.

The younger of the two men followed his question with another. "Who are you?"

"My name is Laura." The two of them looked at each other with a confused expression.

"I'm Ezekiel. Ezekiel Turner." A Turner. Christine spoke of the evil that existed within the Turner family. I was trying to make sense of it all. My mind racing to figure out a way out. "Are you bleeding?"

Ezekiel was pointing to blood on my shirt. I had no idea how it got there but it wasn't coming from me. I shook my head no.

The older man put his arm under my shoulder. I tried to push away before realizing he was only trying to help me to a seated position. "My name is Leroy. Leroy Davis." He wasn't a Turner at least. "Are you sure you are okay?"

The answer was no. I had lost my childhood friend, saw a new friend stabbed and still feared for my own life. I nodded my head anyway.

"Laura, my mom, Margaret, is missing. Have you seen her?" I could see the concern in his eyes.

I have never met Margaret. I have a feeling Christine was involved. "No. I don't know a Margaret. I'm sorry."

Ezekiel's head dropped. Leroy took my attention back to him. "Have you seen Christine?"

This was going to be more difficult to answer. I don't know their intentions and I don't know if they will blame me.

"You have seen her." Leroy interrupted before I could respond. "You paused. You didn't before but this time you did."

My bottom lip started quivering at his tone and insinuation. I couldn't take this anymore. The questioning, the fear, I wanted it all to be over. "She was injured." I dropped my head before continuing, "she didn't make it."

Leroy fell back on to his backside at hearing the news. He looked like he had been punched in the face. He came to after being staggered and responded, "Where is she?"

Ezekiel was now reengaged in the conversation. I used my head to direct the two of them to the cave opening.

Ezekiel stood up over me. "If Christine is down there, maybe my mom is too."

I looked up at him and shook my head as more tears began streaming from down my face. "I don't know."

Ezekiel looked in disbelief. He pulled a pistol from inside the belt of his pants. It had been covered by his untucked shirt.

The tears stopped. Everything stopped.

"Ezekiel, put the gun away." Leroy commanded the younger man to acquiesce.

"I think you know more than you are telling us. I just want to find my mom. I think you can show us the way." He quickly pointed the gun towards the cave opening before returning it in my direction. Tears were now beginning to fall from Ezekiel's eyes.

Leroy tried again, "The others can come and help. They are at the Commune now."

Ezekiel smiled through the tears that ran down his cheeks. "You're right. They will come." He pointed the gun in the air and fired off two shots.

The suddenness of the action caused me to shuffle back as my ears began to ring. The sound carried through the woods. The walls of the Commune close enough to hear the shots. Close enough that others will arrive soon.

"She has been through too much Ezekiel. She doesn't have the strength to…" Leroy was cut off as Ezekiel brought the still smoking gun closer to him.

"And what about my mom? She is to be left somewhere never to be found?" He continued to wipe away tears with his free hand. He grabbed my shirt by the shoulder and pulled me towards the opening.

"Ezekiel, I'm begging you. This is not the way. This is not what your mom would want." He was pleading now on my behalf.

Ezekiel needed the entire sleeve of his arm to wipe the residue of his tears from his face. "We're going. You first." He pointed the gun back at Leroy. "If she falls, you will be there to help catch her."

Leroy gave me a defeated look as he crawled to the opening. "I will help you down."

I put my hand on my mouth in disbelief that I was going back through the arduous journey through the caves. I felt my heart would surrender if asked to do it again.

Leroy put his feet into the hole and began to move down. His eyes were the last thing I saw under the brim of his hat before he disappeared completely. Ezekiel's head followed him over the edge as he looked down the opening.

He turned to me. "Your turn."

I shook my head which caused him to lunge at me.

The gun inches from my face as he pushed me from behind. I could smell the powder from the previous shots.

I tried to grab handfuls of grass around me, but it ripped away from the ground as I slid forward. I was moving closer and closer to the edge of the abyss.

I turned on my stomach as my feet fell into the hole. My hands scratching and clawing for anything around me to grab hold.

I felt a hand on my back gather up a bunch of my clothing. Ezekiel was now kneeling beside me dragging me to the opening. "Please stop." I pleaded with him.

I heard the unmistakable sound of a gun being cocked. He is going to shoot me if I don't move.

"You heard the young lady." It was another voice. "Stop."

My head turned to see a man standing over Ezekiel. The light shrouding the frame of his body. He stepped forward casting a shadow over my head. It allowed me to see him. It was Jack. His gun pointed at the head of Ezekiel.

"Drop it." Ezekiel immediately complied and crumpled into a fetal position. It didn't last long as Jack wrestled his hand free and cuffed his wrist behind his back.

He picked up Ezekiel's weapon and threw it deep into the woods.

Jack's hand stretched out to me as a smile spread across my face. He gently lifted me off the ground.

I put my arms around him like I did six years ago on his porch. The feeling was the same.

He kissed my head. "Laura, I never stopped thinking about you. Every single day. I'm getting you out of here, now."

Jack shouted down the cave entrance. "Leroy, you okay?"

"Yeah. Go ahead. I can climb out."

Jack took my hand and turned to leave the woods.

"Stop." I pulled back on his hand.

"Laura, others are coming. Some friendly and maybe some not. We have to go." He looked confused by my actions.

I let go of his hand after his grip released. I nodded once to him and turned back to the opening of the underground cavern. I took a few steps closer. I was now standing beside Ezekiel. He was lying on his side with his hands cuffed behind him.

I reached down and grabbed the bag by his side. "Now we can go."

I took Jack's hand again and he led me through the woods. We heard the footsteps of others racing to our previous location. Jack had his gun in his left hand in case we met any further resistance.

"Where are we going?" I asked as our path seemed to meander with no sense of direction.

Without looking back, Jack responded, "My truck. It's near the south end of the trestle."

I moved to the front and smiled at him. "Let me." I knew the woods. Every inch. I knew the fastest routes. The routes Billy and I would race through as kids.

My legs felt lighter. I was pulling on Jack to keep up. Weaving and bobbing through the branches. Crunching through the brush as we made our way to the train tracks.

I raced up an incline and stopped as the two of us stood on the elevated track. Ahead a few steps, the elevated trestle. I looked at Jack. "Never again."

We were already on the south side of the trestle that ran to Louisville. We slid down the other side before continuing our run through the woods.

Jack seemed impressed with my leadership. As much spunk as I had shown, the toll was beginning to affect my body. I fell against the passenger side door of his truck.

Jack quickly moved in and helped me into the seat. He raced around and shut the driver's side door behind him. The turn of the ignition fired up the motor and covered the natural sounds coming from the woods.

Intermittent shouts were coming from the two-way radio as Jack made his way to the road.

"Jack! Do you read me? Jack!"

I looked at him wondering if he was going to respond.

He smiled and brought the radio to his mouth. "I read you Wags. I'm good. And I'm retiring again. Over."

The shouts came back even louder once he released the button.

He turned to me and smiled. He tossed the radio to the floor of the truck and switched it off.

Chapter 23: Words

I moved my head over to Jack's shoulder as he pulled onto the road. I felt safe again.

"I have a few questions for you." Jack voice strained as if his age had finally caught up to him.

"I have one for you."

He knew the question. "Yes."

One word. It filled me with joy. Mom was still with us. I was going to get to see her again.

"How is she?" I asked knowing the answer was likely going to be hard to hear.

The hesitation spoke volumes. I could hear him swallow before he replied. "She's not well Laura. Much the same as when you last saw her. She's been unresponsive since the day you left."

The rollercoaster of feelings swung to a new low.

"We did have a moment though. A couple of years after you went missing. I was going through my case files at her bedside. She responded. I can't believe it has been two years since that day."

I gripped Jack's arm a little tighter. "Responded to what?"

Jack took his right hand off the wheel and wrapped his arm around me. "The name Billy."

He had sensed I would need to be consoled. A tear fell from my eye as I thought of Billy.

"He's real, isn't he?" Jack broke the silence with what I assumed was one of his many questions.

"He is... His story and the story of his mom's life both captured in these letters." I pulled the bag to my chest with Jack still holding me.

A moment went by before Jack asked another question. "Is he dangerous? Did he hurt you?"

I took a deep breath before answering. "He was never dangerous to me. He saved my life. Twice."

Jack seemed taken aback at the response. "There are reports. Accusations. Even first-hand witnesses. They talk about him as someone that has harmed others."

"I don't think that is my Billy." I hoped the answer was enough to satisfy the whole line of questioning.

"It sounds like he meant a lot to you." I appreciated Jack changing the direction of the conversation. I was beginning to feel like I was being deposed.

"He did. I have only had a few special people in my life. You being one." I squeezed his arm again to physically show him how I felt. "Billy had less. Only me for most of his life. I always understood him. Understood how the loneliness affected him. I think it is why we needed each other so much."

"I don't know how to say this to you Laura. You mean as much to me as anyone in this world. I did not allow people in my circle. I opened my arms to you when you were ten years old. You were like a daughter to me. Still are. But I have lived a life protecting people from harm. If what the others say is true. If you were Billy's closest friend." He paused between each statement, building towards the words he knew I did not want to hear. "He is all alone. He's out there in the woods. He has harmed others before, and it seems likely, with you gone, that he will again. I can't sit back and allow that to happen."

A few more tears rolled down my face and onto Jack's uniform shirt. "You don't have to protect anyone else. You did your job. You are bringing me home. Everyone is safe now. Billy died this morning in the caverns next to his mom."

Jack tilted his head to where it rested against the top of mine. He knew how much Billy meant to me. I will never see him as the monster everyone else makes him out to be. I know the real Billy. The young boy disguised by his abnormalities and tormented by the environment in which he was raised. A protector that sacrificed everything for his best friend. The real monsters cast his mom and him aside. Forced both to the underground as their only means for survival. If he is evil, it was their actions that made it so.

Jack held me in silence the rest of the way. I nearly fell asleep in his warm embrace.

The turns became familiar to me. I began to reposition myself to see over the dashboard. The sign for my mom's home was passing by the side of the truck. My hand went to release the seat belt as we pulled into the parking lot.

Jack smiled at my excitement. I know this moment is something he had envisioned for a long time. The crowning achievement for a man that spent his entire career serving others.

He slowed the truck to a stop. "Wait." Like a gentleman, he raced around to open the door for me. He knew my legs would be wobbly from the physical and emotional stress I had endured.

We walked side by side as we entered the Sunny Day Senior Center.

Ms. Johnson screamed out as we made our way through the foyer. "I cannot believe my eyes!" Her hands went to her face as the shock set in.

She stood motionless behind the check in counter.

Jack released his supportive grip on my shoulder to allow me to approach her on my own. I extended my hand and placed it on top of hers. It was now resting against her hand which was still pressed to the side of her face. I smiled at her.

Indecipherable sounds released from her mouth. I know she wanted to convey her joy, but the words escaped her. She leaned into the countertop to steady her gait.

"Mom." She knew the reason I was there. She just couldn't believe I had returned after all these years. I removed my hand from hers and reached for the guest sign in clipboard.

Ms. Johnson grabbed the other end of it and threw it over her shoulder. It created a loud disturbance in the usually peaceful office area. We both smiled in unison this time. "Go." It's all she had to say to get me moving.

Jack repositioned himself next to me. He anticipated the strength I would need to walk the hallway to her room.

Ms. Johnson scurried around from behind the desk to follow us. There was no way she was going to miss this.

Each step, I thought of every memorable moment I had shared with this woman. I thought about the unconditional love she showered on me through the years. It meant more to me now. I saw the same depth of feelings Christine had for Billy. Christine forgave her child for his indiscretions. I hoped my mom would extend the same understanding to me. The daughter that left her despite her protest.

We all came to a stop as we reached the room. Ms. Johnson placed her hand on the back of my shoulder. She gave me a nudge towards the door.

I turned to Jack before entering. "What if she doesn't remember me?"

Jack's eyes rolled around as if he was searching for the right words to share. They landed looking into mine. "It doesn't matter Laura."

This wasn't the reassuring statement that I thought he was going to share.

"You remembered her." My eyes widened as he finished his thought. It's all I needed to step forward and go to her side.

The door swung open slowly as my fingertips separated from the surface. Mom was facing the window on the other side of the room.

I tiptoed to the bed as quietly as Billy maneuvering through the woods. I placed my hand on her shoulder and applied enough pressure to turn her towards me.

Would I see anything in her eyes? Would I get any response at all?

Jack and Ms. Johnson had made their way inside the room. Mom was now lying on her back.

I sat down on the edge of the bed and brought my face to hers. I gently kissed her forehead, "It's me momma, It's your Laura."

I brought her hand to my cheek and rubbed it against the warmth of my skin.

I looked into her eyes and could see through her like before. There was still the emptiness in her gaze.

I smiled anyway and closed my eyes. It was a miracle that I got to be by her side once again.

Time came to a stop. We remained in the same position.

I felt a tingling sensation on the side of my face. Mom's fingers began to move. I slowly removed my hand hoping she had the strength to keep her arm extended. I kept my eyes closed as her fingers began to inch their way to my hair line. They nestled between locks of hair caressing the skin beneath. I felt more pressure on the back of my head. She was pulling me towards her.

I opened my eyes. Mom was looking back at me. Her eyes were different. They seemed full of life. Her pupils less dilated. Diminishing the darkness as the colorful ring expanded.

Our bodies met as I fell into her softly. Her fingers continuing to knead the back of my head. Gently tugging and pulling on my hair follicles. I turned to the side to see Jack and Ms. Johnson across the room. My face resting on the chest of my mom. Jack was now holding Ms. Johnson the way he held me as we walked down the hall. Ms. Johnson still had her hand over her mouth in disbelief.

Mom began to whisper at such a low level I could not make out her words. I raised up and returned my full attention towards her. I looked at her in a way that hopefully expressed my eagerness for her to continue.

I brought my ear close to her mouth. I wasn't going to miss another word.

Her light breaths warmed every fold of my ear.

She gathered enough oxygen in her lungs to express the words again. "I love you."

Chapter 24: The Courier

The Courier – October 1st, 1997
Sheriff's Office Raids Property in Shelby County

Details are still being gathered regarding a distress call this past Tuesday to the Shelby County Sherriff's Office. Witnesses reported multiple police agencies responded over the next few hours. The property is home to the Divine Commune, a religious sect founded in the early 1900's by the patriarch of the family, James Turner.

Shelby County Sheriff, Chris Wagner, declined all interviews. The only statement from his office is the property remains under an active investigation. Officers responded from Jefferson and Spencer counties at the request of Sheriff Wagner.

Attempts to gain access to the property were thwarted by the local authorities.

One officer did speak to us under the condition he would remain anonymous given the sensitive nature of the information. He shared at least one individual on the property was found incapacitated and unable to be revived. He also said multiple witnesses have been detained and arrests are imminent in connection with several major crimes that were discovered during the raid. The officer would not release the names of those involved since the investigation is still ongoing.

The County Coroner arrived on scene potentially corroborating the officer's statement.

The Courier – October 2nd, 1997
Identity of the Dead Body Confirmed in Shelby County Raid

As reported yesterday, the Shelby County Sheriff's Office, in coordination with several other agencies, raided the Divine Commune property in Shelby County. The Sheriff's Office released the name of the individual, Simon Turner, who was found unresponsive at the scene. The cause of death is still being investigated. The police are treating his death as a homicide pending further tests.

Elijah Turner, Simon Turner's younger brother, was taken into custody on unrelated charges. Sources have reported that several other people of interest are missing in connection to the death of Simon Turner. The alleged missing persons include the youngest brother in the family, Jeremiah Turner, and his wife, Margaret Turner.

The Divine Commune was once a thriving congregation. The church erected on the property in the 1920's to meet the needs of the growing community. The membership however declined the past four decades as it became more insular from the outside world. One former church member blamed the decline on the change in leadership. "I don't want to trample on anyone's grave, especially a holy man, but the truth is the church was never the same after James' death.

The sentiment seemed to be the consensus of those we spoke to at the Town Diner. A once promising faith-based entity now entrenched behind a wall. Unable or unwilling to attract new members, the congregation devolved to mostly family members living on the property.

The Courier – October 5th, 1997
Missing Girl Returned Home after Five Years

Laura Perry, originally of Shelby County, went missing in 1992. Several verified reports have confirmed she recently returned home to her family. Her birth name was Laura Wilson before being adopted by Jean Perry in 1981. A massive search was conducted in the months following her disappearance. The case became inactive a few years ago when no new leads surfaced.

Shelby County Sheriff Chris Wagner shared very few details when news of Laura's reappearance began circulating. "This woman has been through so much over the past five years. Please respect her privacy and the privacy of her family during this difficult time."

The Sheriff would not elaborate on where she was for five years or the circumstances that lead to her return. He did commend former Shelby County Sheriff Jack Conway for his relentless commitment to the case that resulted in her return. He went on to say it is good to close a case with a positive outcome.

The Sheriff has faced intense scrutiny for the raid on the Diving Commune property earlier this week. The Sheriff would not confirm if there was a connection between Laura Perry being discovered and the raid on the property.

Attempts to contact Ms. Perry or Jack Conway have been unsuccessful.

The Courier – September 9th, 1999
High School Senior Killed on Train Trestle in Shelby County

Jefferson and Shelby County police and EMS responded to an incident on the elevated train tracks off Pope Lick Road. Reports have confirmed the identity of the young man that was killed at the scene. Aiden Sampson died after being thrown from the apex of the train crossing.

Multiple deaths have occurred at the site over the years as curious teenagers and myth hunters search for the infamous goat man. Carly Brooks, a friend of Aiden's, remained on the hillside as Aiden attempted to cross the expanse. She tried several times to get him to come back. She moved away hoping he would follow her to their vehicle. "He just kept walking forward. I don't know why. He never looked back. By the time I turned around, he was disappearing into the darkness. He seemed like he wasn't himself. He wasn't running or nervous or anything. Just walking slowly away from me."

The family has asked for privacy during this difficult time. No charges are expected to be handed down in the latest fatality to shock the rural community.

Chapter 25: The Porch

The only reason I drive into Shelby County nowadays is to visit Jack. It takes a lot to get him off his porch and I figured he has earned a little rest and relaxation. My hands still shake to this day when I drive past the trestles. I never look anymore and yet I can feel its presence. It has been two years since Jack rescued me. So much has happened since that morning.

I have seen Dr. Willis regularly to help me cope with the transition back to a normal life. He was particularly supportive when mom passed away earlier this year. I am thankful for the extra time I was able to spend with her. I consider every minute a gift. A gift I almost never received.

Jack knew I started dating a friend I met at my new job. It all happened so quickly. He finally got the courage to ask me out for dinner six months after I started. We haven't gone more than a few days since without seeing each other. It culminated last week when he asked me to marry him.

My visit today is a special one. I will ask Jack if he will walk me down the aisle. He always thought of me like a daughter. I hoped he would give me away as if he were my dad. It would mean so much to me. I consider him to be the only family I have left.

All the pleasant thoughts made the drive seem shorter than usual. It also kept my mind off the nearby trestle.

His house looked as impeccable as ever as it came into view on the left. Jack was already outside rocking in his favorite chair. He raised his hand to acknowledge my arrival as I turned into the driveway. I playfully pressed the horn causing him to spill some of his coffee. I get him every time. The jarring sound was in great contrast to the serene country setting. I could see why it startles him. His smile let me know he didn't mind the disruption. Afterall, he doesn't get many visitors.

I brought my car to a stop and leapt from the door before the engine quit running. Jack was shaking his head as I approached.

"You still haven't learned how to slow down have you." He chuckled as the words left his mouth. I knew he never sat still when he was my age. Heck, up until he rescued me, he was still going a mile a minute. Age and worn out knees are the only things that have slowed his pace.

I gave him my normal elongated hug before sitting in the chair beside him. He already had a glass of lemonade sitting on the bench for me to drink.

Jack had trained me to sit still for a few minutes. To take in the view and breathe in the fresh air before speaking. It was difficult this time given the news I had to share. I finished off the drink to satisfy the time requirement. The clock ticking in my head as Jack stared directly ahead. I couldn't help but notice he seemed to be thinking of something else. He has something to share and I get the feeling it is not good news.

"Jack. I have to ask you something today." He continued looking ahead as he took a sip of his coffee. I reached over and put my hand on his arm. "Jack?"

The physical contact caused him to turn towards me. He placed his other hand on top of mine. "I'm sorry Laura. Go ahead."

I'm not sure if I had his full attention. He still did not seem present. Regardless, I hoped my good news would cheer him up. "I'm here about Brandon." He barely nodded reinforcing his protective outlook on everything I shared. Brandon came with me a couple of months ago. I wanted the two of them to meet. Brandon was quickly becoming someone very special to me. Jack's approval is all I needed to give my heart completely to him. Jack played the role of dad extremely well. He made sure to point out his gun collection as he showed Brandon the house on our last visit. We weren't there long when the two connected. Brandon had served in the army before going to college. The two of them spent an hour sharing stories of basic training and the camaraderie they had with the people they served beside. I was an afterthought for most of the conversation, but it didn't bother me one bit. "Brandon asked me to marry him." I fell to my knees and placed both my hands on his arm.

It took a few seconds before a smile broke through his tough façade. "I'm happy for you. I truly am. Why are you kneeling?" He laughed again. I believe he was doing anything to keep from tearing up.

I looked up at him, "because I would like for you walk me down the aisle."

He lifted me up off my knees and held me close. My chin resting on his broad shoulders. His hand gently pressed against the back of my head. He was doing anything to keep me from seeing his reaction. "I would be honored." He managed to get the words out somehow. The quiver in his voice confirmed the emotions he was harboring.

Our embrace lasted several minutes until both of us had a chance to collect ourselves. We fell into our chairs causing them to rock faster than normal.

More time passed as the morning crept along on his front porch. He never talked incessantly on my visits, but the silence was extreme even for a man of few words.

"Jack. What is it?" It was time to give him the floor. Whatever was weighing on him needed to be said.

He bit his lip as if he still wasn't sure he wanted to share. "There was another incident at the trestle since your last visit." He trailed off at the end. We never spoke of the trestle, the woods or the Commune. We both pledged to move on and put that chapter of our lives behind us.

I looked to the other end of the porch not sure I was ready to hear anymore. "And?"

"It didn't get reported. The details. The witness accounts. I'm not sure why Sheriff Wagner continues to share them with me. I think he believes I know more than I am letting on." His rocking slowed and along with it the creaking of the wood slats beneath us.

I turned back to him. "Did you tell him about Billy?" I waited anxiously for his response.

"I gave you my word to..." His sentence cutoff mid thought.

His smile now erased from his face. He seemed disappointed in me.

"Jack. I thought he was dead." It was true. When I left, Christine was ready to end it. I didn't like to think about it. Deep down I always hoped he might have survived.

"They found evidence Laura. Evidence that would incriminate him in this latest incident." He looked lost like a sailor being thrown off course by a storm.

All the nervous feelings I had managed to keep at bay came rushing back. "Do they know about him?"

He shook his head. "No, but I do. I know I promised not to tell, but I cannot allow him to hurt anyone else." He turned his attention directly to me. "What really happened out there? They never found the rest of the bodies. Jeremiah and Margaret are still legally missing. Teams searched miles and miles of the caves and never discovered anything below the surface. They eventually gave up with no one pushing for answers and limited resources."

The excitement I felt for the wedding had completely subsided. My head dropped to my hands. "I thought he did die. You must believe me. When I left, his mom, Christine was going to take her son's life and her own. Christine is the reason I was able to escape and meet you under the trestle. I thought it was over."

Jack placed his hand on my shoulder bringing my head up from my hands. "Christine was Billy's mom? She had a son?"

I nodded. "Yes. It's all in the letters. Her entire story. I still thought it was over. She was tired of fighting."

Jack was now rubbing my shoulder. The last thing he ever wanted is to see me upset again. We had so many good visits on his porch over the last two years. I thought all of this was behind us. It all changed with another death on the trestle. A death he feels responsible for not stopping.

"I talked to Christine." I leaned towards him having no idea the depth of their conversation. "I did. The night before I took you out of the woods. She never mentioned a son. She was continuing to protect him. Protecting him like you are still doing to this day." He was talking through it out loud like he was investigating a case.

"What now? What will you do?" I feared what he might say.

He changed the subject. I knew what that meant. He started to talk but my mind was already thinking about his next steps. Jack will go back into the woods. He will hunt him down. He will do everything he can to bring him in. Except he won't. He can't. Billy is strong and agile. If he survived, as they say he has, he will kill anything or anyone that crosses his path. Everyone except me.

My thoughts were disrupted as I caught the last few words. "Did you say Christine's dad is still alive?"

He looked at me like I hadn't been listening. "Yes. Or at least he was two years ago. I didn't know she was Billy's mom."

"Christine didn't know. Why didn't you tell me?" I pleaded with him.

He looked away embarrassed by his omission. "All I can say is I wanted to protect you. Wags was asking so many questions. You remember those first few weeks after the raid. I saw how you left each interview. I tried to distance you from any other entanglements. Christine would have opened a whole new investigation. I always thought they would find them. When they did, the truth would come out. All of it except your involvement. It all went away as time passed. They stopped asking questions. Christine was never a focus of the investigation. She has vanished from ever existing. I couldn't deliver the unfulfilling news to her dad. He had a lifetime of getting used to her being gone. How could I tell him that his daughter has been alive all this time? Is he supposed to be comforted knowing she may still be out there and suffering? It wouldn't be closure it would be heartache all over again."

I stood up and positioned myself behind his chair. I realized Christine's dad was just like my mom. Waiting for answers. Waiting to fill a void that had tormented them for years. They both needed a resolution no matter how devastating it may be. It is the only way you can truly grieve and ultimately find some peace. "We have to try. We can do it together. He deserves to know what happened to his daughter." I put my hands on his shoulders.

His hand moved on top of mine. I saw the brim of his hat move up and down ever so slightly. "I need to make a call."

He stood up and went inside. I sat down in his chair and awaited his return. I pictured Christine's face. She may be the strongest woman I have ever met. Her frail stature masking the will she had to raise her son in the worse possible environment.

He came back on to the porch with a jacket in hand. "A man answered the phone at his address."

"You called him?" I couldn't believe he would have the conversation without involving me. "Did you tell him?" I stood up across from him waiting to hear his response.

He shook his head. "It's not something you share over the phone. You still have the letters?"

I nodded.

"Then let's go to Huntington."

Chapter 26: Huntington

We sat in silence most of the three-hour ride. I clutched the bag holding the letters the entire time. I thought about the journey Christine made to Louisville 33 years ago. She traveled a similar path in the opposite direction. A decision that forever changed her life.

"Why do you still own the property on Pope Lick Road?" Jack interrupted my daydream.

I have never lied to Jack. Anything I said, would stretch the truth at best. I kept the property for one reason and one reason only. Billy. My silence only raised Jack's frustration with me. He didn't know Billy like I did. You can piece together the stories and not fully realize what he endured. Surviving childhood alone was a miraculous achievement. "What's happened to the Divine Commune." I diverted the conversation away from Billy.

Jack paused not sure he should share anything with me that might upset me again. "I think you're ready. You have earned the right to know what happened to those involved. The property has been vacated. I saw a for sale sign posted a few weeks ago. Thomas and Ezekiel were the last to leave. Elijah is in prison for a multitude of charges. Several others served time as well. There was so much evidence incriminating everyone at the Commune. All of them were guilty of something. All of them had blood on their hands."

Christine's actions brought it all down. The whole church. It all crumbled under the weight of the lies that had been hidden for decades. She was an inspiration.

Jack pulled off the expressway. It wouldn't be long before we were at her childhood residence. My mind shifted to the conversation I was about to have with her dad. There are no words to comfort a man who never got to see his daughter grow up. He never got to see her graduate or have the honor of giving her away. He never even met his grandson. What words would give him peace.

I didn't have to use my words. I had Christine's. I pulled the letters out and began flipping through them. I had read them all many times. I stopped on one of the many letters Christine had written to her dad. The words brought both a tear to my eye and smile to my face.

I looked up to see we were turning into a subdivision with quaint houses lining the street. Jack glanced at the map, "one more street."

He turned on the cul-de-sac and slowly idled forward. His hands straining against the steering wheel of his truck. The house sat directly ahead. He glided the truck into the driveway bringing it to a stop.

We both sat still looking directly ahead. Another pick up truck was parked in front of ours. He must be home.

I reached for the door handle, but Jack grabbed my arm. "You can't just go up there and hand this man these letters." I looked at him like he had three heads. I thought that is exactly why we made the trip. He reached into his console and removed his old Sheriff's badge. He pinned it to his shirt. He lowered the rearview mirror to make sure it was straight and presentable. "You know I am going to have to tell Sheriff Wagner about our visit here."

I wasn't concerned about Sherriff Wagner. I wasn't even concerned about Billy. I was concerned about Jack. "Will you get in trouble?"

He turned to me and looked me directly in the eye. "Laura don't ever let the consequences keep you from doing the right thing. The only regrets I have in my life are when I compromised or justified my actions." While I appreciated the life lesson, it did little to avail my concerns. My expression clearly displayed his answer was not enough. "I'll be fine."

Jack reached for the door as I stretched out to stop him. My hand glancing off his sleeve as he pulled away.

I sat up in the seat and watched him approach the door of the ranch style home. I imagined Christine sitting in her car the day she backed out of the drive for the last time. Her dad's smile masking the anxiety he felt inside.

The image of a typical dad standing on the front step was replaced by an older man that stepped out from the house. He moved beside Jack as they exchanged pleasantries.

I leaned in pressing my forehead against the passenger side window. I could not make out any of their words. Jack motioned his arm over to the truck which brought Mr. Ferguson's eyes in my direction. I sheepishly raised my hand just about the console.

Mr. Ferguson acknowledged my gesture by raising his hand as well. His face carried the burden of a man that had been suffering for years. Jack nodded to him and began walking back to the truck.

I sat back not knowing any of the conversation. Neither of them giving anything away with their stoic expressions.

Jack came beside the passenger door and pulled the handle. I nearly fell out as my fingers were dug into the arm rest of the door.

Jack spoke softly to me. "He's ready for you. You can tell him everything."

I collected the letters and placed them back into the bag as tears began to fall from my eyes. I held the one letter close to me and took a deep breath.

"Laura." Jack spoke again. "I know this is difficult. He is going to need you to be strong. Strong like his daughter. Show him the same strength."

I wiped my eyes as I nodded back to him. "Okay." I sat the bag of letters on the console between the two front seats. The piece of paper in my hand is the one he should read.

Jack helped me down from the truck. I was standing on the ground, but it didn't feel like it. The first few steps felt like I was trudging through six inches of mud. Mr. Ferguson watched me as I approached the porch.

"Good afternoon Mr. Ferguson." I smiled to ease the tension.

A small smile quickly came and went on his face. "Laura? Is that what the Sheriff said is your name?"

"Yes. Can we sit down." I moved my head in the direction of the porch swing.

Mr. Ferguson remained quiet as he turned towards the swing. I glanced back at Jack who was now leaning against the front of his truck with his arms folded in front of him. He gave me a nod of encouragement.

Mr. Ferguson allowed me to sit first. He was a very large man. As he awkwardly lowered himself, the swing began to move in all directions. I wondered if the old wood swing and chains would support the two of us.

Both of us placed our feet on the ground to stabilize the swing. He took up over half of the seat causing his side to rest against mine. He seemed self-conscious of both his size and the physical contact.

I placed my right hand on his left arm. "I met your daughter. I met Christine."

He began to shake as he buried his face in his left hand. The swing rocking even with our feet planted on the concrete porch.

"She wanted so much to get back to you. She was misled to believe you had died. I know she would have fought to get back here if she knew you were alive." I was doing my best to control my emotions. It wasn't easy given his reaction.

I squeezed his arm with a little more force.

It took him a minute, but he finally put a few words together. "I would have given anything to talk to her one more time."

I closed my eyes and thought of my mom getting to share so much with me before she passed. "You cannot talk to her, but she can talk to you."

Another minute passed as he collected himself. "What do you mean?"

"She was talking to you all along. She wrote it down." I place both hands on the letter that was resting in my lap. "She kept you alive in her letters, which in turn gave her another reason to keep going."

He was still shaking as I handed him the letter I chose from the pile. I had to carefully place it in his hand given how unsteady his arm had become.

The words were bouncing up and down as the tears continued to fall from his eyes. He was squinting and opening his eye lids to clear his vision. He lowered the letter to his lap and looked up to the roof of the porch enclosure. "I… I… Would you read it to me?"

He looked away from me as he moved the letter to my side. I didn't expect this. I wanted him to hear her voice. The voice he remembered when she was just sixteen. I took the letter from his hand. I am not sure why I moved closer to him. I placed my head on his shoulder. His arm moved and wrapped around me. I remember reading how Christine loved his big bear hugs. I could see why she enjoyed them. I felt like I disappeared nestled in beside him.

I brought the letter up and read his daughters words to him.

"Daddy,

I see you on the porch every single day. Waving to me as I leave. You were with me all this time. I never stopped thinking of you.

But it was more than that, everything you instilled in me as a child is how I managed to live. You gave me the strength to endure.

I wish I could have told you this myself. It is very important for me to say this to you. It wasn't your fault. I lied to you. I went somewhere that I shouldn't have, and you knew better. You were only trying to protect me. So, it wasn't your fault and it wasn't all bad.

I fell in love. It was fleeting but it was love. I know now that it was the real thing even if it was only a few hours. His name was Johnny Wallace."

Mr. Ferguson was shaking more as he tried his best to keep listening. "Johnny."

"You knew him?" The way he said it implied as much.

Long pauses interrupted his sentences. "He came around a week or so after Christeeny left. He had seen the press releases. The papers helped us get the word out regarding her disappearance. We spent an entire year searching. He was a good person. Christeeny gave her love to a deserving man. We kept searching but it was like she disappeared from the earth. I finally got him to go back to school. He needed to start living again and stop searching in the past. I never stopped searching. He still calls once a month to check on me. He always ends the call by asking about her."

I exhaled. It was beautiful and tragic all at the same time. I allowed some time to pass before finishing the letter.

"You would have liked him dad. He was smart and funny. I believe he would do anything for me. I know I didn't know him long, but I knew who he was, and it just felt right.

After Johnny, I learned how to be a woman. I made a couple of friends. Margaret and her son Ezekiel. Together, we helped each other. I wasn't alone.

I had one more person in my life and that was Laura." As much as I wanted to read the letter clearly this part always caused me to choke up. She had penned the letter the night before she poisoned Simon. "Laura took care of someone very special to me. She helped me to know the right thing to do when the time came. I gave her my story knowing my life had purpose. I helped her. I gave her the inspiration to get back to her life. Back to the people she loved. And I knew she would take my story with her and I would live on through her." The tears fell from eyes as they fought through my restraint. Mr. Ferguson was now comforting me.

"It's clear you meant a lot to her." He rubbed my shoulder and took the letter from my hand. "I am glad she had you…" He was unable to finish the sentence. The emotions too intense to overcome.

He took the letter from me. I closed my eyes as he finished reading her words. "I leave here knowing I was always loved. Unconditionally. I know you forgave me for my decision, and I know you would wrap your arms around me if I somehow managed to get back to you before you were gone. I believe I will get to see you now. I believe good people get to be reunited when they leave this place. So, I am not sad daddy. I am happy that I will be in your arms soon.

Love, Christeeny."

Chapter 27: The Promise

Before I left, Mr. Ferguson gave me one of the hugs Christine had spoken so fondly about. The tears were gone from his eyes as he stood on the porch. He would alternate glancing at the words on the page and back to us as we sat in the car. He smiled as he placed the letter against his chest.

I looked to a window of the small house as we backed out of the drive. I wondered if it was Christine's. I pictured herself standing there as a teenager full of hope and dreams. Wishing with everything inside of her for the rain to stop. If only the rain would end, she could see Johnny again. I imagined a smile spreading across her face as the sun pierced through the clouds.

We were both silent as Jack guided us back to the expressway.

I could have gone the entire three hours without talking. My mind jumping from Mr. Ferguson, to Christine's journey, to Billy, and the life I had in front of me with Brandon.

Jack broke the silence. "Why didn't you give him the rest of her letters?" The bag was still sitting between the two of us.

There were two reasons. Only one I could share with him. "The other letters talk about abuse. They talk about fear. I know how painful that is to endure. I didn't want her dad to read those words from Christine. The letter I chose expressed her love and her hope. It's what I needed. It's what he needed to hear." The other letters also talked about Billy. A grandson that he never had a chance to meet and never should.

I wasn't sure how Jack was going to receive my answer. He was a principled man. As much as he thought of himself as a rebel, he was a product of his training. A rule follower. A person that never let emotions determine his actions. It served him well all these years.

"You know Laura. I have just one thing left that I have to do." He put his hands on the bag of letters.

He is going to report them as evidence.

He lifted the bag and placed it in the space behind my seat. "I have to walk you down the aisle."

"Would that be doing the right thing Sheriff." I smiled at him.

He unpinned the badge from his shirt and placed it on the dashboard. "It is, for you." His arm stretched out behind my head rest.

I moved to the middle and secured the center safety belt. I positioned myself against his side. A sense of relief came over me.

Made in USA - Crawfordsville, IN
81286_9798632011808
06.22.2020 0452